YET I STILL
STAND

A NOVEL

STEVEN WAYNE

iUniverse

YET I STILL STAND
A NOVEL

This is a work of fiction. All of the characters, names, incidents, organizations, and dialogue in this novel are either the products of the author's imagination or are used fictitiously.

iUniverse books may be ordered through booksellers or by contacting:

iUniverse
1663 Liberty Drive
Bloomington, IN 47403
www.iuniverse.com
1-800-Authors (1-800-288-4677)

ISBN: 978-1-5320-4710-7 (sc)
ISBN: 978-1-5320-4711-4 (e)

Library of Congress Control Number: 2018905115

Print information available on the last page.

iUniverse rev. date: 05/17/2018

Dedication

To my lovely and intelligent daughters, they
taught me how to laugh again.
Aliesha Nicole
Kiana Marie

In loving memory to my beautiful, warm hearted,
and best friend, I miss you so much.
Christie

To my editor, she provided sound guidance and
perfect recommendations, thank you so much
for your commitment to my manuscript.
P.N. Waldygo of Desert Sage Editorial Services

To my readers and benefactor, I appreciated
your honest review of my project.
Lynn (NeeCee)
Melanie

To my parents, they started me on my way, with love and guidance.
Leo Earl Jr.
Gloria

Acknowledgement

O nly words printed on this page can describe my sincere adoration for you. For over 30 years you have imbued me with an unconditional love. But through it all, every morning I could see your beautiful face and every night I could hold you tight. So, I thank you for your support and encouragement. When I wanted to give up our battle cry became *"just finish the rest will take care of itself"*. Love you always my wife Lorie Ann.

"Because I was a young, naive little boy, I never contemplated or worried about that time in my life when my innocence was so abruptly taken away from me. I know a lot of kids had a rough time growing up, but now I'm still tortured by childhood demons. I wish this pain would go away. I wish I could walk away from this miserable feeling of hopelessness. I wish I could love my life again. I want to die! I don't want live if this is how I'm going to feel all the time!"

ONE

"Touchdown, he scores!"

The yells of adoring fans rang in Jonathan's ears. His imagination ran wild. He paused to do his famous touchdown dance, while his teammates cheered him on.

"Go, Johnny, go! Go, Johnny, go!"

"Hey, Jonathan, are you listening?"

Tyrone shoved him into the fence they were walking past, ruining his fantasy.

"What's your problem?"

"You're my problem, punk."

Jonathan dropped his bag and positioned himself to fight Tyrone. There had always been bad blood between them. Once Tyrone's older brother Trey had beaten Jonathan up for no reason at all.

"You wanna dance?" Jonathan asked.

"Bring it."

"Stop it," Steven said. "You boys, knock it off."

Jonathan picked up his bag and the football.

"So, are we going or what?"

"What? What did you say?" Jonathan ignored Tyrone and continued to toss his football up in the air, as Tyrone repeated his question.

"I said, are you coming to the park with us? We're gonna play football with some guys from P.S. 274."

"Aw, man, I have to go," Jonathan said. "See you guys tomorrow."

"Yeah, come on, man," Ray added, "they won't even know what hit them."

"Nah, man, I wish. I have to get to the house."

He heard grumbles from his crowd of friends, but they were used to this by now.

"You always have to go. What's up with that?" Steven complained. "They don't love you anyway. Come on, just one game."

"Or . . .," said Ray.

"Or what?" Tyrone said.

"Or we can go to his house and fuck his sisters," Ray said. "Especially Gail, with her fat ass."

"Shit, yeah! Let's get some pussy."

"Hey," Jonathan said, "If you have sex with them, I personally guarantee all of your body parts are going to fall off and rot, because they're some of the nasty bitches."

They all laughed.

"Your dicks will burn into a pile of black ash. The pain will be so bad that you'll want to kill yourselves," Jonathan continued. "Anyway, I can't, guys. But next time, I promise!"

He tossed the ball to Steven, who ran and caught it with one hand.

"See you tomorrow!"

Tyrone, the leader of the group, was big for his age. Any time you needed something done, he was the man. Jonathan didn't like him or his brother Trey. They were gradually becoming hard-core drug dealers.

Ray was the quiet one, but he had deathly fast hands. It was very rare that he got into a fight, but when he did, the other person got beat almost to death. Boy or girl, he didn't care.

Alan had a big mouth, always talking about some bullshit.

Steven was the singer; he had a great voice. He and Jonathan were the smartest of the group, and they were best friends. He was short, similar to Jonathan. They both were around three feet, two inches, and maybe forty pounds, and most boys their age were over four feet tall.

They belonged to a gang started by Tyrone's brother Trey, called the Lil' Trouble Makers. Although Jonathan didn't lead the group, he had a lot of influence when it came to making decisions about the trouble they got into.

Jonathan took his time walking back to the house. He didn't really need to rush, because he hated being at that house. He never called it home. It was only a house to hang in until he was old enough to move out.

Jonathan took after his father in being short, but he believed he would be over six feet tall when he grew up, so he didn't stress over his height or weight. When he heard other kids talk about their siblings, he wondered what he'd ever done wrong in life to deserve such horrible sisters. They were all older than he was, and the only one he really cared about was Nina. He could count on her to have his back. The rest of them could burn in hell, for all he cared.

His mother was even worse. She was always drunk and smoking cocaine. She stayed up for four to six days at a time. He didn't care much for her.

His father was a wannabe gangster and an extremely angry person who felt he had to act like a jerk to gain respect and recognition from others. Jonathan figured he was compensating for his short size. He was shorter than most of the guys he hung around with. He had a Napoleon complex or short man syndrome. He gave away money to everyone just to please people. He was overly aggressive, a mobster, but Jonathan thought he was a complete asshole.

Jonathan didn't like his father. He believed that his dad should protect him, not call him names. Jonathan knew he took after his father in many ways, but he prayed to God that he wouldn't end up like his old man. He knew, deep down inside, there was a great person within him. He would make a name for himself one day.

"Hell, yeah, I am Jonathan Anthony Russo," he stated proudly.

Three girls passed by and giggled when they heard his boast. He felt tempted to chase after them.

Aside from football, that's another thing Jonathan loved—he loved the girls. Yet it had taken him awhile to want to be around them, because he thought they were all like his sisters. Happily, he discovered, at the tender age of eight, that other girls were different. He liked all types of girls: tall, short, light, dark, skinny, and even some of the fat ones. He loved them all. As he watched them walk past, he felt himself start to grow hard. He cringed at how uncomfortable it was, and he couldn't wait to get home to take it out of his tight uniform pants.

He didn't have a care in the world. He was a very loving and trusting little boy. He got into trouble, as most young boys did, but he loved life. He couldn't wait to wake up every morning and see what he could get into that day, just living one moment at a time. He hit puberty at the age of eight. He got erections all the time but didn't know why. He didn't dare ask his parents, because he loved his new toy so much. He knew his parents would destroy his fun. He believed that some things were better left unsaid.

Jonathan's hormones were out of control. He got excited without any stimulation at all. He would hump anything and anybody, the wall, the floor, the edge of the bed. He always dry-humped girls in the stairwell at school. He would have fucked dogs if he could be sure they wouldn't bite him in the ass.

He never asked his parents about sex; he figured he could learn as he went along. He just knew that whenever he saw a pretty girl, it happened. Then he would feel things. He couldn't describe how it felt. It was a need, so strong that sometimes he wondered how he controlled himself around girls. There were times when Jonathan got lucky, because girls thought he was cute. They would go with him to the fourth-floor staircase and kiss him all over his face. He didn't really like kissing, but he put up with it so that girls would let him hump on their legs. They always giggled, and he enjoyed himself.

One day on the way home from school, a voice in his head told him to walk a different way, but he ignored it. All he could think about was how many times his father had drilled it into his brain, which way to walk to the house so that he would get there on time. If he ended up anywhere else, it would be his own fault, and he would be in trouble again. Jonathan didn't want to hear his father's shit today. So even though something told him not to walk his usual way, he ignored it. His father's voice overpowered any other feelings he had. He shook off the feeling and kept walking.

When he saw the creepy abandoned house, he knew he was almost home. Jonathan and his friends called it "Ghetto Ghost Alley." He was all too familiar with that place. If anyone wanted to join the Lil' Trouble Makers, the boys put a football in the backyard, and you had to run as fast as you could to get it and make your way back without falling. If you could do that, then you had what it takes to hang with their crew. If someone didn't make it, the guys usually just beat him up. There were absolutely no girls allowed. Trey was the true leader of the Lil' Trouble Makers, and he told the boys he was grooming them for greater things.

When Jonathan finally made it past the abandoned buildings, he noticed a tall girl standing not too far away. He wondered why she was there by herself. She wore a similar uniform to his: a white top, blue pants, and blue shoes. But, then again, most schools in the area had the same uniform. As he got closer, he thought she was somewhat cute, but he had no intention of stopping and talking to her. When he tried to walk past her, though, she jumped in front of him.

He tried to move out of her way.

"Where do you think you're going?" she asked.

"Why?"

"'Cause I asked, that's why."

He took a minute to stare at her. He had seen her around, but she wasn't anyone important or special to him. She was tall with long black hair and was a little older than he was. She had an adorable smile, but he didn't like the color of her eyes. They looked amber or yellowish, golden with a russet and copper tint.

They seem to be evil, he thought.

She had a cute face, and she looked very familiar to him. She gave him a slight smile that in his eyes could be deemed predatory if she were a grown woman.

"Hi," she said, before he had a chance to step around her. "Hey, boy."

He gave her a slight nod and made his way around her. She grabbed his arm.

"Wait!" She smiled again. "You want to come with me for little bit?"

"No. I think I should go!"

"Come on, it will be really quick, stop being a pussy. I want to go in there." She pointed to an abandoned building.

Oh, shit, Jonathan thought. *Ghetto Ghost Alley!*

Jonathan knew he was cutting it close to the time he was supposed to be back at the house. Yet he'd always wanted to go into those buildings. It was the chance of a lifetime, and the good thing was, he had a girl with him. At this point, he felt as if there was no choice.

He nodded, not trusting his voice to speak because he was nervous. He would never admit to anyone that he was scared, especially to his friends. They would never let him live it down.

She snatched his sweaty hand and held it tight. He noticed that she didn't even hesitate as they climbed the steps into the yard, but his nerves felt shattered.

They walked through the gate and up to the front door. She stopped for a second to look around, then pushed open the rickety door. Sunlight streamed from the few windows that weren't boarded up tight.

She shut the door and led him to the middle of the room. Then they walked up the wobbly stairs, with her leading the way.

Without warning, she let go of his hand and pushed him. He fell down the stairs and landed on his back, dropping his backpack.

She ran to get him and grabbed his hand. She looked around, but she wouldn't let go of his hand.

Jonathan threw a punch at her, and she was able to block it. She slapped him in the face. She didn't say a word. They started back up the stairs again and headed into a dirty room, painted lime green. A filthy mattress lay on the floor.

She looked at him and demanded, "Put down your bag."

"No!"

"Is that all you can say?" she questioned.

"I don't think we should be here."

"You will be where I tell you to be. Now shut the fuck up, and put down your fucking bag! Don't make me ask you again, or I'll kick your ass!"

She punched Jonathan in the chest. He fell back and hit the floor. She lifted her leg and kicked him in the chest. When he tried to get up, she kicked him again. He watched her, trying to think of his next move.

Something made Jonathan pause for a moment before he did what she said. He was about to ask what they were going to do when she interrupted him.

"Okay, now what?" As he eyed the mattress, he thought that he would rather jump out the window than sit on it.

She instructed him to get off the floor. "Lay down."

"What?"

"Lay down. Why do I have to keep repeating myself? Fuck, lay the fuck down now, and if I have to repeat myself again, I'll kick the shit out of you! Don't make me hurt you."

"Then what?" he asked. But for some reason, he complied and sat down.

She knelt over him and started undoing his pants. His mind finally kicked into overdrive, and he realized he wanted out.

"No, no, stop. I don't want to."

"Shut up!" she said, interrupting him. "You don't have to do or say nothing. Just be a good boy, and do what I tell you to."

He tried to get up, but she held him down. He bit his lip to keep the tears from falling, more out of fear than anything else. He didn't know what was about to happen. He figured she was obviously crazy. Once she got his pants to where she needed them, dangling around his ankles, she took off her pants and panties. Suddenly, there was a smell so strong he had to fight to hold back his vomit.

"Do you want me to take my top off?"

What the fuck? he thought. *This bitch has the fucking nerve to ask me that shit. Fuck her.*

She took her top off, even though he hadn't answered her. He didn't know what to do, so he prayed that it would be over fast, and he could get out of there. He closed his eyes, pretending that he was in a football stadium in front of ninety thousand people, scoring the winning touchdown.

"I don't want to do this," he said.

"What? You just lie there and enjoy."

She slapped him in the face repeatedly. He couldn't block the blows because her knees were pinning down his arms. He didn't say another word.

Her body had an odor of rotten dead fish that quickly saturated the air. He felt sick from the stench. He again fought the urge to vomit. He still refused to open his eyes. Feeling and smelling her was enough for him.

Jonathan was furious. He wanted to pick her up and throw her out the window. He truly looked at her and could see the evil in her eyes.

He pulled away from her and saw large patches of blood going from his stomach area. He looked at the bed and saw fresh blood on the mattress.

Unable to hold back his vomit anymore, he turned away from her and heaved.

They both ran out of the building.

Damn! That bitch didn't even ask how I'm feeling, he said to himself.

"If you ever tell anyone, I will hunt you down and kill you," she said.

"Whatever. Fuck off. My sister hits harder than you."

Jonathan ran to the house. His hands shook while he opened the door. He finally made it inside, where he dropped his things and ran to find his mother.

"Where the hell have you been?" she screamed.

"Wait, let me tell you, Mommy, please listen!"

"I told you to stop calling me Mommy. You call me Ms. Anna, and I'm not your fucking mother!"

Jonathan pulled down his pants to show her the blood.

"What the fuck is that? Take your nasty ass into that bathroom and go wash. You stink! Get out of my face."

His eyes widened, and he was on the verge of tears. Nevertheless, anger took over. "Please, I think you should hear this."

"What did you say to me? When you start working around here and bringing money to the table, then you can make requests. Go wash your ass. End of story. I don't want to hear whatever bullshit excuse you have for coming in here with blood all over you."

"But, Mommy—"

"I'm not going to tell you again. Go away, you stink."

Dismissed, just like that. He stayed in the shower for a long time because he felt dirty. He should have expected her not to listen or understand. He wanted to tell someone he needed help. He couldn't understand why his mother wanted him to call her Ms. Anna. He decided that he would never talk to another girl again. After a hot shower, he went straight to bed.

"Fuck these bitches, fuck them! Fuck them!" He went to sleep with that thought in his mind.

Then he had a nightmare. He was running and screaming but couldn't wake up. A white light shone down from the ceiling. Jonathan became paralyzed as the light pulled his lifeless body up to the ceiling.

This scared him. As he struggled to move, he heard a deep voice: "You are not ready yet."

The light flipped him over, and he opened his eyes and saw his body lying on the bed below. Then he saw a green light glowing on the bed. He tried to pull away from the white light, and he could feel the green light pulling him down. The white light became brighter, then let him go.

When he hit the bed, he woke up.

Bewildered, he thought that maybe yesterday had also been a dream, part of the nightmare he'd just had. But it wasn't.

When Jonathan got up, he didn't have the usual spring in his step. He didn't eat breakfast that morning because he felt so ashamed of what had happened. He put his books in his backpack and went to school. Normally, he walked to school with his friends, but today he wanted to be alone.

As he approached the school, he started getting queasy in the stomach. He felt nauseated and alone. He went to his usual spot in the playground and sat there. His boys came around and asked him what was wrong, but he decided that he couldn't tell them.

When the school bell rang, Jonathan glanced over and saw the girl from yesterday. He moved closer to where she was playing, and one of her friends called her name: Lisa. He burned her face into his memory.

She walked away, but, to Jonathan's surprise, she turned her head and winked at him with her evil eyes.

He was terrified.

TWO

S till upset from two days ago, Jonathan needed to talk to somebody, anybody. He decided to try his older sister Judy, but he knew deep down that it was a mistake.

Jonathan's stepmother, Ms. Anna the bitch, and his father didn't talk to him much, and they never did things together as a family. His father would go out with everyone except Jonathan. His family was involved in a business they didn't want him to know about. The boy didn't know what his family did or why they never invited him to go anywhere with them. He believed that Ms. Anna and his father cared more about his sisters than him. He was on his own a lot and felt very lonely at times.

Judy was the oldest sister, fourteen years older than Jonathan. She was a very serious girl. She liked to fight, and she always carried a gun.

Jonathan knocked on Judy's door, and she invited him into her room. He despised her, but he was hurting. Before he could say a word, his sister started yelling at him.

"You're not coming in here to tell me some bullshit story, are you? Because I don't need that right now, so tell me what you want, and get the hell out of my room."

Jonathan didn't understand why everyone treated him so badly. He lost control. All he wanted was for her to listen to him.

"Fuck you, bitch!" he screamed.

Judy jumped out of the chair and, with all her strength, punched him in his arm with the speed of a skilled boxer. He couldn't let himself cry—he didn't want to give her the satisfaction.

11

"You talk to your little fuck-face friends in the street like that, not me. Don't you ever curse me again!"

Jonathan couldn't take it anymore. "Get the fuck off."

Judy kicked him and said, "Welcome to manhood. Now who's the bitch? Get the fuck out!"

She got off him and kicked him again in the chest.

Jonathan slammed the door on his way out, thinking of all the confusion in his life and how lonely he felt. He decided that to survive, he had to take charge of his own life.

He went to his room and lay in bed with tears in his eyes, thinking about life. He wondered how a ten-year-old boy could take charge of his own life. To him, it was all philosophical bullshit. The only thing he knew was to try to do one thing, and if it didn't work, do something else.

Later that afternoon, Nina came into his room and sat on the bed. She was the only sister he cared about.

She touched his forehead. "Hey, John John."

"Hey."

"What did you do to Judy?"

"I wanted to talk to her."

"Why did you yell at her? You know she's a crazy bitch. She's going to kill you one day. You hear me?"

"Bullshit, not if I don't—"

"Shut up, don't say it." She covered his mouth with her hand. "Come look at me. What happened?"

He turned his head and looked at her. He loved Nina, but he couldn't be sure whether he could trust her. He told her about Lisa and the things they did.

"People . . . sometimes they take things that are not theirs."

"I don't understand why Lisa would hurt me."

"I don't know. But I do know that people are fucked up at times. You'll be okay. Don't let people destroy your spirit. We'll never know why people act the way they do."

Jonathan looked at Nina and grabbed her hand. She kissed him on the head.

"Hey," she said, "don't you know you just got some bad pussy, that's all."

"What?"

"Listen, you're going to find some girls are just foul. They don't know how to clean themselves."

Nina explained a woman's body to Jonathan. She showed him more than he probably needed to see. She went into his bathroom, wet a towel, and cleaned his face.

"Listen, rest, and in the morning life will still suck, but you'll be fine, okay?" She kissed him on the lips. "I love you."

"Love you, too," he said.

Jonathan got up the next morning with new hope, but now he had another dilemma: dealing with the family dogs.

They were Doberman pinschers, one named Thunder and the other, Lightning. Those dogs were monstrosities. Thunder, a black male, weighed about 165 pounds, and Lightning was a 140-pound red female. They both were four years old.

His father told stories about how the dogs had special powers and could speak to each other. He claimed they were born killers and would kill anyone, if their master ordered them to.

They were from Florida, descendants of Jason the Warlock. They were probably the smartest dogs in the world. Jonathan's father talked about those dogs all the time. To Jonathan, the dogs were a major pain in his ass, and if he could have, he would have killed both of them. He was sick of the dogs intimidating him every day.

Jonathan knew he couldn't tolerate the dogs much longer. They were always around, controlling him. Anytime he was in the bathroom, they hung around the door. When he ate, they would team up and take his food. One day Jonathan was eating a hamburger, while Thunder watched him. In one smooth motion, Thunder snatched Jonathan's burger out of his hand. The dog walked away with his food.

When Jonathan went to sleep, the dogs walked around the house, patrolling the kingdom. His father had total control over them. Jonathan had seen Thunder and Lightning kill cats, birds, and dogs, and one time they chased an ant into an anthill. Those dogs dug up the ground and destroyed the whole colony.

They never bothered his sisters, though. In fact, the dogs were deathly afraid of them. One night Jonathan's sisters had trapped Thunder in the basement and beat him near to death.

Jonathan knew that at some point in his life, he had to stand up for himself. Thoughts raced through his head. He kept thinking about that incident with Lisa. He couldn't get it out of his mind. He still felt as if nothing would ever be right for him again.

Yet somehow he survived the week. He enjoyed watching cartoons on Saturday morning and drinking cola before he went out to play. It helped pass the time and cleared his mind.

One day while Jonathan was watching television, Lightning walked into his room. Jonathan sat on the floor, relaxing. The dog walked to the corner of the room, turned around, and then walked out.

A few minutes later, Thunder and Lightning both came back to his room. Jonathan knew something was getting ready to go down. Lightning went to the far corner of the room, near his bed.

Jonathan looked around and started planning an escape route.

His living area had three rooms: the bedroom, the bathroom, and a walk-in closet. As Lightning watched Jonathan, Thunder walked toward him.

Thunder barked at Jonathan, and the boy got up and moved out of the way. Thunder barked twice more, and Jonathan sat back down.

He said aloud, "This shit has been taken to another level."

He had an empty soda bottle in his hand. He wished he had the strength to hit the dogs and kill them both.

He'd complained to his father repeatedly about these dogs, but his dad really didn't care and always just told him to grow up.

Jonathan looked at the window and calculated how he could get outside without the dogs following or biting him. Every time he changed positions on the floor, Thunder growled at him.

Those dogs terrorized Jonathan. They bullied him. He was a prisoner in his own room. He realized that he needed to protect himself because nobody would do it for him.

Lightning started pacing the floor.

Jonathan got more nervous and gripped the bottle tighter. He looked at Thunder.

"Leave me alone."

Thunder growled at him, grabbed his arm, and held on tight but didn't break the skin.

Jonathan yelled, "Leave me alone!"

Thunder let him go.

Jonathan sat next to the wall with tears in his eyes.

He watched Thunder dripping slobber all over the place, and, for the first time in a few days, he no longer felt helpless. He dried his eyes and stared at Thunder. Lightning left the room, and Jonathan knew this was their pattern of attack. He knew he had to come up with a plan soon.

He looked over at the television, then switched his attention back to Thunder. The dog had started to relax a bit, because Jonathan could see Thunder's little red dick getting hard. It looked like a red snail, wet and slimy, sliding across the floor.

Jonathan saw an opportunity and gripped the bottle as tight as he could. He raised his arm high, and with all of his strength and power, with every hate-filled emotion that he felt for his family, all of the anger he felt for his sisters, rage at every action that was taken against him, he smashed the bottle down on Thunder's dick. He held the bottle on Thunder's penis until it was almost flat.

Thunder's body convulsed violently, and the dog stopped breathing. Then he let out a loud yelp.

Jonathan stood up, took the bottle, and hit Thunder in the head.

He screamed, "Where are your fucking special powers now?!"

He knew that dogs could not shed tears, but he would have sworn under oath that he saw tears coming out of Thunder's eyes.

Lightning came running into the room to see what was happening. Thunder kept yelping and trying to get off the floor, but Jonathan hit him again under the chin, as blood dripped out of his mouth.

Thunder got up, and Jonathan took the bottle and hit him in the nose with so much force that Thunder spun around and pissed on the floor. Thunder tried his best to get out of the room to leave, but Jonathan did the unthinkable and kicked him in the balls. Thunder collapsed on the hardwood floor, while Jonathan stood over him like a lion over its prey.

He shouted again, "Where are your special powers now?!"

Lightning stood there without moving, watching all of this unfold, and then Jonathan started howling like a wolf. Lightning put her ears down, and Jonathan prepared himself to deal with her.

"Come on, bitch, all of us are dying today!" he yelled, without any hint of fear in his voice.

Lightning leaped at Jonathan, and he hit her with the bottle. He backed up a little and kicked her in the chest.

Thunder managed to get to his feet, Jonathan kicked him in the balls a second time, and Thunder shrieked and fell to the floor again. Lightning backed down.

Lightning went over to Thunder and grabbed his collar to help him up. As Thunder was leaving Jonathan's room, the dog turned his head and looked at Jonathan. Thunder's facial expression said, "Why did you do this to me, man?"

Thunder walked away a broken dog, and with every step he took, he cried out in agony.

Jonathan proudly roared, "Who's the bitch now?!"

He heard them both go down to the basement. About an hour later, Jonathan went downstairs and saw the dogs sitting quietly in the darkest corner of the basement.

He went back upstairs to the kitchen and cooked some chopped beef and rice. When he returned to the basement with the food, he didn't see the dogs. He found them hiding in a hole behind the water heater.

"You can come out, but if you attack me, I will kill you both."

They cautiously came out of the hole, and he gave them the food and watched them eat.

"Hey, I guess nobody should take an ass whipping like that!" Jonathan said.

He thought that the dogs might take revenge, because if it was the other way around, he sure would. But instead, both dogs walked over to him and licked his face, and he rubbed their heads.

"You know, we're going to be okay."

The dogs went back to finish their meal.

Thunder and Lightning never bothered Jonathan again. When they saw him coming, they greeted him with affection as if he were their new leader. There was no more harassment.

Jonathan became the new alpha male and the dogs, his best friends. He thought about what he had done and realized that his actions and conduct had to be respectable, for him to receive the benefits of being respected.

There would be consequences for his negative actions. However, he believed that sometimes it was essential for his actions to be brutally forceful. He had to cause bodily harm, to the point that the person had a near-death experience, in order to gain that individual's respect. Jonathan had earned those dogs' respect by using force.

THREE

I t was about ten o'clock, the morning after Independence Day. The sun was shining. It was another wonderful day. Jonathan sat in his room, talking to the dogs. They listened to his every word. Following his command, they performed each task to perfection. He trusted those dogs with his life, and he proudly walked the street with them.

He felt ready for a great summer of fun, sun, and sitting around with his boys, eating and playing football all summer long. He'd received top grades in junior high, and he was going to an all-white high school in the fall to play football.

Two years had passed since his encounter with Lisa, and he couldn't shake the feeling that she looked like someone he knew. He hadn't come to grips with what had happened. It still frightened him from time to time, especially in his dreams. But other things in his life were going well: he was developing a relationship with his sister Nina, and he'd made great progress with the dogs.

Jonathan's father, Frank, opened the bedroom door.

"Who are you talking to?"

"The dogs—we're just playing."

His father said, "Got them under your control, boy." Then he laughed.

Jonathan hated his father for not being there for him. "No, they're your dogs. We're just playing."

Jonathan was lying, of course. He had the dogs under his control, and he was the alpha male.

"I want you to go to Toledo, Ohio, to see your grandmother."

"What? I'm going by myself?" Jonathan asked.

He didn't like the news, because he had plans for the summer. He paused, turning his attention away from the dogs.

His father didn't care for Jonathan's tone of voice. He pointed his finger at the boy. "I don't want any shit from you. Your sister is going with you."

Jonathan knew this could only mean Nina, because the others would never be seen in public with him.

"But I don't want to go."

"I said no shit. Judy's packing your bags."

"Shit! Okay."

Jonathan was pissed off that he had to leave New York. Judy walked into his room, acting like her usual queen bitch self. She looked around the room, got his bags, and started to pack.

"You big pussy," she said. "Get outta my way."

Jonathan didn't want to get into a fight today, so he moved aside and watched her.

After Judy packed, she gave him the bags. "Have a safe trip, asshole, and if the plane crashes, I hope you're the one that dies."

"Fuck you," Jonathan said.

He took his bag and went outside, where he saw Nina. Jonathan called her Trixie, but only in private, never in front of his other sisters, and she called him John John. He loved her because she treated him nice. His other sisters would beat on him and call him terrible names.

"Have a safe trip," his father said. "See you in a few days."

The other seven sisters kissed Nina and walked away from Jonathan. He didn't care. He hated those bitches anyway. Judy kissed Nina and punched Jonathan in the arm.

He ran back to the house and went into the basement to the weight room. He saw Tommy and Rico working out with weights. He told them he was going to Ohio to see his grandmother. They wished him a good, safe trip and gave him four thousand dollars to spend. He put the cash in his backpack and went back outside. They got into the car and drove off to Teterboro Airport in New Jersey.

"Why are we going to Ohio?"

"To see our grandma. I heard she is dying and wants to talk to you."

"About what?"

"I don't know. I heard she's just a crazy old lady. I'm just going to keep you out of trouble and then hang out."

"The story of my life—I'm surrounded by crazy ladies."

Nina laughed. "You don't know how true that statement is."

Jonathan got sleepy on the way to New Jersey, and Trixie let him put his head on her lap. Before he fell asleep, he felt her warm legs on his face, and it felt comforting.

"Hey, baby." She kissed his cheek. "Get up."

At Teterboro Airport, they were greeted by a man named Rick. He didn't speak, he simply handed Nina some papers. Jonathan expected Rick to take the bags, but he didn't. Rick told Jonathan to take their bags to the airplane.

Jonathan was excited to see that it was a private jet. When he got on the plane, he felt so happy that he jumped from seat to seat. "This is what I want."

"Hey, let me give you some advice," Rick said. "Always act like you been there before, okay? So, calm down."

"Okay."

At times, Jonathan could be as playful as a little boy, but other times, he was like a sophisticated man ordering single malt scotch in a cocktail bar in Monaco. When the plane reached flight altitude, the captain asked Jonathan to come up front. He spent some time with the captain, who explained the different instruments. The captain told Jonathan that he could tame anything with the right training. He gave Jonathan his wings and wished him good luck.

The flight lasted about one hour. When they arrived in Toledo, a driver was waiting to take them to the University of Toledo Medical Center.

Jonathan had never been in a hospital before. This was all new to him. Nina held his hand as they walked through the halls of the hospital, escorted by a doctor. When they reached their destination, Jonathan saw his grandmother in bed.

"Hi, Grandma."

She opened her eyes and put on her glasses. "Hello." She held out her arms. "Come give Mama a hug."

Jonathan ran to her and hugged her tight.

"So you're Jonathan, the only boy in the family. Such a lovely young man. Who is your friend?"

"That's Nina."

"Hi, Grandma."

"Hi," his grandmother said.

Nina told Jonathan she would be back in three hours, and the doctor and Nina walked out of the room. Jonathan climbed onto the bed and held his grandmother for a few minutes, then sat next to her on the bed.

"Boy, you're so little."

"I'm going to be tall someday, not short and fat like my father. I'm going to be a great football player."

"Or maybe a great protector."

"We'll see." He shrugged.

"You are the only boy in our family in a long time."

"Okay."

"Do you want anything?"

"No, not really." Jonathan didn't know his grandmother, but he felt heartbroken to see her in pain. "I'm fine."

"Aren't you happy to see me?"

"I guess."

"Why are you so unhappy?"

"Really, I'm fine. What's your name?"

"Aiyana."

"Nice. If I have a daughter, I'm going to name her Aiyana."

Aiyana smiled and said, "I want to tell you something."

"What?"

"First look in the closet and take out the box and open it."

Jonathan jumped off the bed and went to the closet, where he saw a brown box. Inside, he found a gun.

"What is this?"

"It's a gun. I want you to have it."

"Why?"

"I own it, but I want you to have it. Come here."

Jonathan walked to the bed with the gun in his hand. "Show me how to work it."

"It's not a toy. Tell me you understand."

"I understand. So it's real?"

"Yes, it's real. It's a Smith and Wesson .357 magnum. It has a three-inch barrel."

"I don't have a clue what you're talking about, Grandma."

She handed him some papers. Jonathan opened them to see a land deed in his name for seventy thousand acres in Montana. She also gave him a key for a safe deposit box.

"Take it. The instructions are for your eyes only. The things in that box are only for you, and the bag is for my brother Duke. Keep this secret. You can keep a secret, right?"

Jonathan thought about the first real secret he was keeping. Once he went into the basement to get his jeans out of the clothes dryer and heard weird noises from the other room. He walked over to the exercise room, opened the door, and saw Tommy and Rico having sex. Rico was on top of Tommy. In all of the books he'd read and porn films he'd watched, he'd never viewed two men having sex. Jonathan tried to close the door, but Rico saw him. Rico stopped, put a towel around his waist, and chased Jonathan until he and Tommy caught the boy. Jonathan wanted to run, but they were too big and fast. Tommy told him never to say anything about what he'd seen. He made Jonathan promise and gave him five thousand dollars.

Tommy and Rico, both white men, worked as his father's bodyguards. Tommy's full name was Michael Thomas D'Azzo. He was a highly decorated detective with the New York City Police Department and had been awarded the Presidential Medal of Honor. Rico K. Alamo had been on the police force for ten years. Jonathan didn't know why they worked for his father, and he didn't care.

Jonathan wasn't concerned about what they did, but if his father, Frank, ever found out, he might have killed them, and Jonathan felt very sympathetic to Tommy and Rico's situation.

After that day, Tommy and Rico took Jonathan everywhere, taught him to drive, and gave him everything he wanted. They always gave Jonathan money, and for that, he never told.

"Yes, I can keep a secret, Grandma."

Aiyana explained the family history to Jonathan. His family was from Cetona, Italy, a town in the southern part of the province of Siena, in the region of Tuscany. His grandfather was Frank Paul Russo Senior, but they called him Frankie P. He had moved from Italy to Montana and married a Blackfoot Indian named Aiyana. He'd moved to Brooklyn, New York, and had ten children, nine girls, and one boy, Frank Paul Russo junior. He was the youngest, and they called him Frankie J. The family grew up very poor. Frank Senior made his money as a gambler. He was considered a very good poker player. His problem was that he cheated. It caught up with him, and he was shot ten times for cheating in a card game. Those shots killed him.

Frankie J married Anna Maria, an Africa American beauty queen and a former track star from Brooklyn, New York. She had lived in the Marcy Housing projects, located in Bedford – Stuyvesant, Brooklyn, New York. They moved to Queens and had seven children. Judy was the oldest, then Gail, Anna, Maria, Paula, Taren, and Alicia, the youngest.

Frank was a gangster in Queens, New York, because that was all he knew. He was a gambler, and he owned a brothel in Freeport, New York. Frank was a master of his environment. People feared and respected him. He always got what he wanted when he wanted it. He knew the system and made many people rich.

Jonathan's grandmother said that his father had other children and that his real mother was named Brenda. Also, she had three daughters: Lisa, Kara, and Sandra. His grandmother continued, telling him that he had ten more sisters: Kia the oldest, Tina, Diana, Chelsea, Jada,

Joan, Melissa, Ariel, Linda, and Sandra. Their mother was named Karen.

"That's your family: twenty girls and one boy."

"So now I understand why she makes me call her Ms. Anna."

"Don't worry. One day you will see your real mother. You are a very special boy."

"Thanks, Grandma. What's up with Nina?"

"Listen, I know you don't know this, but Nina is not your sister. Tommy is her father, and Anna is her mother."

"No shit!"

"Hey, watch your mouth."

He smirked. "Sure, Grandma."

"I am dying. I'm happy that we had a chance to talk. Don't forget to read all of the papers. Also, see my brother Duke in New Jersey, his number is in the letter, and give everything in the lock box to Duke."

"I totally understand, Grandma. I love you, Grandma."

"I love you, too."

Nina came to pick up Jonathan, but they didn't talk much. They called for room service, ate dinner, watched television, and then went to sleep. The next morning the phone rang in the hotel room. It was Jonathan's father. He told Jonathan that his grandmother had passed away and to be ready in one hour because "you and Nina are going to Montana for the funeral."

"I just spoke to Grandma yesterday," Jonathan said.

"Son, that's the way life is. I want you to handle this for me. Just go with it; we're not going."

Jonathan thought his father was wrong to stay away from his own mother's funeral. "I'm not sure what to do."

"Just be there," his father said.

Jonathan really didn't know what to expect from the trip to Montana. His grandmother had known she was going to die. She had given him a gun, a deed for seventy thousand acres of land, and a safe deposit key. He wanted to tell Nina, but he kept it to himself.

Jonathan and Nina flew to Billings Logan International Airport and then to Cut Bank Municipal Airport, both in Montana. On the ride to the reservation, Jonathan read the following in a newsletter:

> The Blackfoot Indian Reservation, or Blackfoot Nation, is an Indian reservation of the Blackfoot tribe in the U.S. state of Montana. It is located east of Glacier National Park and borders Canada to the north. Cut Bank Creek and Birch Creek make up part of its eastern and southern borders.
>
> The reservation contains three thousand square miles, half the size of the national park and larger than the state of Delaware. It is located in parts of Glacier and Pondera Counties.

When Jonathan and Nina arrived at the reservation, they prepared for the funeral.

They learned that a spiritual service is always held over the dead body of every Native American, young or old, even of infants who have lived for only a few seconds or minutes. According to spiritual and ceremonial law, when a Native American dies the body must be washed with fragrant lavender and oil to clean away impurities. Then the body is wrapped in a white cotton cloth or a sheet.

The corpse is put into the coffin, and an eagle's feather is placed on the body. Native Americans believe they must show respect for their dead. A qualified Native American chief, shaman, or elder performs the burial rites.

After the funeral, Chief Clayton asked Jonathan if he was interested in doing a vision quest. Most of the men and boys performed vision quests to find out what they wanted to do with their lives.

"Why me?"

Chief Clayton said, "I see something in you."

"What?"

"It's for you to find out. It would not be right for me to tell you."

"Okay. I'll try."

"No, I want you to commit to this," Chief Clayton said. "It is very important. You are the first young man to come into this family in a long time."

"Yes, I'm committed," Jonathan said.

He told his sister, "Nina, I'll be back in four days."

"Hell, no. You are not going into the woods for four days. Not on my watch."

"I have to go," Jonathan said.

"I said no."

"Nina, he will be safe," the chief said. "I have a person who will look out for him."

"No," Nina said. "He has never been in the woods before. If something happens to him, I would die and so will a lot of you."

The chief said, "It will be fine. It will be good for the boy. Trust me."

She looked at the chief and said, "In my world, 'trust me' means 'fuck you.' If you say it's safe, then okay, but if something happens to him, there will be no power on this earth that will stop me from killing everyone on the land. Believe that shit!"

She turned to Jonathan and said, "I love you. Please be careful."

"I will, and when I come back, I'll be the protector of the world." Jonathan smiled, happy that Nina was looking out for his welfare.

"Just be careful, okay? This is not a game."

"Okay. I got it."

"This is Jo, he's going to be your leader," Chief Clayton said. "Follow his instructions. Let us pray first."

A few minutes later, Jo said, "Come," and led Jonathan into the woods.

Jonathan thought to himself that he would ask God for guidance. And to watch over him in this life. For that, he would do his best to watch over others. He wanted to be a warrior.

The first night Jo didn't say much. Jonathan walked by the creek to get some water, where he saw a pack of wolves. They were gray wolves, so he didn't feel any danger. The wolves gathered into a pack and trotted toward Jonathan. He called out for Jo, but Jo didn't come.

Jonathan fell to his knees and prayed, "God, help me, I don't want to die, but if I do, I will always love you."

It was dark and he was in a frozen state. He just didn't move. One of the pups came over to him. It licked his face and smelled him. Jonathan rubbed the pup's chest and then its head. Two more pups approached him.

"You guys stink," Jonathan said.

Three of the old wolves walked over to Jonathan, and he wasn't afraid anymore. He got up from his knees and started to walk. He called out for Jo a few more times and followed the creek. He found a large broken branch, and that became his walking stick.

The next day Jonathan was up for about fourteen hours. He was beat, but he wasn't sure whether he should sleep. He walked along the creek, drinking water and playing with the pups. At night, the pack climbed on top of the highest rock and howled for hours. Jonathan realized that he was alone. Jo had run away, and he was truly alone. Under the full moon's light, he decided to walk along the creek. He took off his shirt and put some mud on his face. He figured this would protect him from the sun the next day.

On day three, he saw a search team looking for him.

A helicopter flew overhead. He waved, but no one saw him. They were searching but couldn't find him. Jonathan knew you couldn't find anything that wasn't moving. The wolves followed him everywhere.

Jonathan felt extremely tired. He wasn't sure what to do next. He decided it would be easier to go back. He jumped into the creek to cool off. He figured it had to be three days because he had seen three moons. When he started to walk back, the pack of wolves surrounded him.

As he followed the creek, he realized that this was truly an experience, and the wolves fell back. Jonathan became the alpha male. He knew that God wanted him to succeed at this. He knew that he would be successful.

He also knew that no matter what happened, he would be the protector of the ones he loved and whoever needed it, and if someone died along the way, then so be it.

Now Jonathan headed back toward the reservation. He saw that the wolf pack had gotten bigger. There had been five at first, but when he counted again, twenty wolves walked behind him.

Jonathan came to the end of the forest. He stood there with the sun at his back and twenty wolves surrounding him. He paused for a second to take it all in, holding the big branch he'd found. He smiled, feeling very happy. He felt empowered.

He said to himself, *Out of the smoldering pit of fear come the fresh cooling waters of courage that give me strength to go on, regardless of the obstacles in the world.*

Jonathan looked at all of the tribe members standing around, as if waiting for something or someone. He commanded the pack of wolves to go, and, one by one, they turned and walked away.

He saw Nina, ran toward her, and hugged her.

"Don't ever do that again," she said.

"I got lost."

"We were very worried about you," the chief said, "but we knew this was not a mistake. It was God watching over you. Be loyal, have compassion, give service, and be a protector, because you're a true warrior. You have the heart of a wolf. Good job."

Kimba, a young native girl, gave him a feather, saying, "This is for you, my hero." Then she kissed him on the cheek. "Job well done."

After Jonathan got hugs and kisses from the tribe, a group of men took him to another room to get cleaned up. Nina followed them, because she didn't trust anyone. She could not bear to lose Jonathan again, so she watched the men very carefully.

During the powwow, Jonathan passed out from complete exhaustion. He woke up in bed in the hotel room, with Nina staring at him.

"Hey, sleepyhead, it's time to get up. You've slept more than fourteen hours. Get up, we should go. It's three o'clock in the morning. We have a six-hour flight."

"On the private jet?"

"Yes." She smelled his underarms and backed away. "You stink. Take a shower."

She kissed him, and he pulled the covers over his head.

"Come on, stinky, I love you for what you did. You can sleep on the plane."

When they arrived at Teterboro Airport in New Jersey, Jonathan saw Rick standing by the plane. The crew took Jonathan's and Nina's bags out of the plane. Nina went to pick up her bags, but Jonathan told her to leave them. As he and Nina walked toward the car, Jonathan turned to Rick.

"Please get our bags."

"You're kidding, right?"

"No!" Jonathan said. "Get our bags,"

"Hey, kid, go fuck yourself."

"Really! No, fuck you." Jonathan pointed at the bags and said, "Get our fucking bags now."

Rick walked back to the plane and got the bags. This was an important turn of events, because Jonathan discovered who he was and who he was going to be.

Nina didn't say anything. She had just watched him grow up.

When they got back to New York, Jonathan went to see his dogs. As they jumped on him and played, he told them about his grandmother and the vision quest. He knew they didn't understand a word he said, but he didn't care.

He went to the kitchen and saw Judy cooking.

"So what, fuckhead, what's up?" Judy asked. "Are you a redskin now?"

"Leave me alone."

"Fuck you and your fucking vision quest."

"Okay, whatever."

He didn't really have the energy to deal with this. He had other things on his mind. He called Duke in New Jersey and introduced himself. Duke gave him directions and told Jonathan he should spend two weeks in New Jersey.

Jonathan told his father he was going to a football camp in Union, New Jersey. His father didn't pay attention, as usual. He asked his father for three hundred dollars, and without hesitation, Frankie J gave him the money. Jonathan told Tommy, Rico, and Nina he would be back in two weeks.

He packed some clean clothes, called a cab, and went to 34th

Street in Manhattan. He wanted to see what was in the lock box at the Midtown Bank & Trust Company. All they asked for was his identification.

When Jonathan opened the safe deposit box, he saw about ten thousand dollars in cash and a small black felt bag, filled with diamonds. A note said, "Please give to Duke. Love, Grandma."

He put everything in his backpack and left the bank.

He looked back and saw people watching him, but he just kept moving, as if everything were normal. Yet there was nothing normal about a twelve-year-old boy with a lot of cash, diamonds, and a gun. He hopped into a cab and went to Grand Central, where he bought a ticket to Manalapan, New Jersey.

When he arrived, he took a cab to Branchburg and found Duke's Gun Shop and Supplies.

"Good afternoon, Mr. Duke, I'm Jonathan."

"Just call me Duke."

He was a tall man with short gray hair. He looked just like Aiyana. Jonathan knew he was from the Blackfoot tribe, but he had a strong Southern accent, which made Jonathan laugh. Duke showed Jonathan around the place and introduced the boy to his dog, a bloodhound named Cory.

Duke said that he'd heard about what happened in Montana and that he was very proud of Jonathan, because their family didn't have many men, and Jonathan was the first in a long time to complete a vision quest.

Jonathan gave Duke the ten thousand dollars in cash and the diamonds. Duke told him that he was an honest man and he could be trusted.

Jonathan didn't need money anyway, because Tommy and Rico gave him money all the time. It was rare for him not to have at least two thousand dollars in his pocket at any given moment. If he needed to, he could easily put his hands on twenty thousand.

Duke taught Jonathan everything about firearms and bomb making. By the time he left, he had become an expert marksman and was able to take care of himself in any situation. It was an intensive two weeks, working fourteen-hour days.

Jonathan could take apart a Glock and put it back together blindfolded. He knew everything about a Glock 9mm and a 357 magnum.

During the two weeks, Duke repeatedly told Jonathan, "Two bullets in the heart and one bullet in the head."

As a parting gift, he gave Jonathan a silencer for his 357 and the Glock 29, extra ammunition, forty blocks of C-4, and body armor.

Jonathan thanked Duke and went back to Queens.

FOUR

It was Jonathan's first day of high school. Because of his excellent grades in junior high, he had skipped seventh grade and was able to enter high school at age twelve. He was only four feet, nine inches tall, and about eighty pounds.

He enrolled as a freshman at Springfield Gardens Preparatory High School, one of the most exclusive private high schools in Queens, New York. He'd been heavily recruited by the Springfield Colts in the high school football league. They gave him a full scholarship to play football, and the school was within walking distance from where he lived.

Jonathan wasn't pleased to go to an all-white high school, because he wanted to hang out with his friends, but if this would get him away from that dysfunctional family and help him get a football scholarship to college, then he was all in.

As Jonathan walked to school that early September morning, with the sun shining, a hint of summer remained in the air. He saw many new faces. He walked along Springfield Avenue, the main street in the town of Springfield Gardens. He walked past the football field and couldn't believe he would play football there soon.

He noticed the other students crossing Springfield Avenue to get away from a gang of about twenty boys, all of them much taller and bigger than he was.

A young girl behind him crossed the street. She yelled at Jonathan to come with her, but he looked at her and got confused. He kept walking, but it was too late. The gang of white boys surrounded him.

"Hey, asshole, this is my fucking street," the leader of the gang said. "Don't you know never to walk this way?"

"What?" Jonathan asked.

"Are you stupid? You can't hear?" another boy said.

Jonathan didn't speak, and he dropped his books.

"Fucking jerk. What are you, fucking tuff?" one of the boys shouted.

"Let's call him tiny, 'cause he a little motherfucker," another white boy said. "Shit, you would never play football on my field, we know who you are."

"That's the ticket, we don't want no blacks in our school," the leader of the group said. "We're going to kick his ass good!"

Jonathan didn't panic. He knew what was coming and just took like a man. The boys rushed him, punched, and kicked him. They pushed him to the ground and kept kicking him. Jonathan could taste the blood from his busted nose. He covered his face and kept saying to himself, *Don't cry, it will be over soon.*

As fast as the kicks and punches came, he saw an opportunity, grabbed a leg, and held it tight. They kicked him so hard, his body contorted, and his iron grip twisted the boy's leg. He heard the sound of a bone breaking and then a scream. Despite the beating he took, Jonathan hung onto the boy's leg. When they finished punching him, he let go of the leg and stood up.

The gang of boys snatched his new book bag and threw it into the street. They laughed at him, called him "stupid boy," and walked away.

After the boys left, Jonathan fixed his pants and brushed them off. He saw blood on his shirt, then noticed one of the boys on the ground, crying in pain.

Jonathan walked over to him. He looked up at Jonathan and asked for help.

Jonathan said, "Fuck you."

He kicked the boy in the face, then several times in the ribs. "This is war. Tell your fucking friends."

The young girl crossed the street and picked up his book bag. She looked at the boy on the ground and didn't say a word, then walked over to him and kicked him in the face.

She smiled at Jonathan. "My name is Sharon."

Jonathan didn't respond right away. She glanced at him, and they both started toward the school. Jonathan paused, then walked back to the boy and kicked him again.

"Tell your fucking friends they are dead."

Sharon and Jonathan headed off to school together.

All day long, students talked about what had happened. They stared at Jonathan in the hallways, astonished that he had taken a beating like that and didn't cry or end up in the hospital. It pissed off the gang's leader, Darrell.

Jonathan heard that Darrell was going to get him the next day for kicking one of their own. Darrell was white, about 220 pounds, a high school senior, and a football star. He hated black people. It turned out that Jonathan had broken the boy's leg, and his and Sharon's kicks had shattered the boy's cheekbone and cracked two ribs.

On his way back to the house, Jonathan saw Sharon. "Hey, wait for me."

She stopped, as Jonathan ran toward her.

"Hi, my name is Jonathan"

"Hey. Are you okay?"

"Yeah, just a little sore."

"Come to my house, it's right over there." While they walked, Sharon brushed his hand with hers and said, "I don't really know you, but you have a problem."

"Really? Because if it's about what happened today, I will kill all of those white motherfuckers, one by one." He shrugged his shoulders.

Her eyes widened. "Shit, so you some kind of bad boy? You're so little. The word is that Darrell is going to make sure he puts you in the hospital."

"Fuck him."

"So, Mr. Bad Boy, you're not scared?"

He shook his head. "Nope, never that, I will deal with them."

"You'll be the first, because nobody would dare fight with them, without fear of being killed. There's a story that he killed a young black boy when he first started the school."

"Killed?"

"No, silly, they just beat you up, over and over, and I heard that you'll wish you were dead. Students transferred out of the school because of what Darrel did to them. His father is a New York State senator. He thinks he's hot shit."

"Fine, I will discourage that shit. Have they ever bothered you?"

"Yes."

"Don't worry, I got you."

"You got me?"

"Yes."

They both smiled.

When they arrived at Sharon's house, Jonathan was surprised at how beautiful it was. He heard a dog barking, and he jumped a little, but she guaranteed that "Tiger is a good boy."

They went inside, and Sharon told Tiger to go to the back room. He gave a low growl.

"Maybe you should wait outside a minute," Sharon said to Jonathan, but he walked toward Tiger, a German shepherd.

He put his hand out, and Tiger walked over and licked it. Jonathan stroked the dog's head, and Tiger trotted to the back room.

"I've never seen him act nice to anyone," Sharon said. "He's a great dog, but he doesn't like anyone I bring over."

"I'm just good with dogs. Woof."

They both laughed.

Jonathan looked around and thought, *What a wonderful house.*

He felt surprised to see everything in its place. He wished it were his home. It had a big television, and the house seemed warm and had a loving feeling. Sharon told him to take off his shoes. He felt comfortable.

"Have a seat, come sit next to me."

"Okay," he said and sat beside her.

"Have you ever kissed a girl before?" Sharon asked.

"Yes."

"So, do you want to kiss me?"

"I don't know."

He was very cautious with any girl he put his lips on, because his first kiss with Lillian Williams had not been a good experience. That girl had made him sick, literally. His throat had ended up swelling, and he lay in bed for days. So, safe to say, he didn't like kissing too much.

"Come on, baby, kiss me," she said, leaning in closer. She was so close, Jonathan could smell whatever spray she used.

"Okay."

He pressed his lips against hers, and they felt soft and warm. He could feel the breeze from her nose. Her lips tasted like watermelon.

Sharon whispered, "Open your mouth."

Jonathan complied, and she slipped her tongue in. He got excited and started to shake a bit, then he moved his tongue inside her mouth, kissing her passionately.

He stopped, looked her in the eyes, and said in a very deep voice filled with confidence, "I got you. Nobody is going to bother us again, and that's a promise. I will be there for you always."

Before she could say another word, he kissed her again.

She heard the front door open and jumped up, then moved to the other side of the couch.

"Hi, Mama," she said with a wide smile.

"Hey, baby, who's your friend?"

"Mommy, this is my new friend Jonathan. Jonathan, this is my mother, Ms. Fleming."

Jonathan stood up and reached out to shake her hand. Ms. Fleming grabbed his hand and moved him close to give him a big hug.

She's a lovely woman and she smells so good, he thought. *Her body's warm.*

"It's so nice to meet you," she said. "We give hugs in this house. You can call me Ms. Renee, okay? Are you okay? I see some blood on your shirt."

"Yes, I'm okay. I got into a little fight with some boys, but I'm fine."

"Mommy, they really beat him up, they pounded the crap out of him, punched, kicked him. Can you take a look at him, please? He got beat bad, but he didn't cry. But he got one of them. He is the talk of the school today, because most people who get beat up by those boys cry all day. Those stupid boys are all going to get it one day. Jonathan got one, and good. That boy is in the hospital. We heard that he got his cheekbone broken and some cracked ribs."

"Okay, baby, you're going on and on. Let me see about him." Ms. Renee took Jonathan by the hand, and they went upstairs to the bathroom. She picked him up and put him on the edge of the sink. He took off his shirt.

"What are these bruises?" she asked.

"From football."

"What? Are you telling me the truth?" She raised her eyebrow.

He simply shrugged. "I don't know."

Ms. Renee stepped back, put her hand on one hip, and looked him up and down. "Were you in another fight before this one?"

Jonathan held his head down. He wasn't the crying type, but Ms. Renee's caring voice got to him. He wanted to tell her about all of the terrible beatings he received from his sisters. He felt more convinced now, after meeting his grandmother, which they were trying to kill him. He was a strong little boy, and he vowed to take care of that situation one day. He wanted to tell her, but he couldn't be sure whether he could trust her yet.

Ms. Renee touched his bruises, and Jonathan flinched because they were sore.

While Ms. Renee attended to Jonathan's wounds, he felt a love that he'd never felt in his entire life. He mumbled to himself, "This is what it must feel like to have a loving mother."

Sharon looked in on her mother and Jonathan. "Mama, he's the new football star at our school."

She looked Jonathan up and down again. "You're so little."

He smiled a little. "Yes, I may be small, but I am good."

"That may be, young man, but if you were my son, no football for you."

After that statement, Jonathan started to cry. He lost control of his emotions and released the built-up stress with every tear that flowed. Although Jonathan was only twelve years old, he felt as if he'd lived a lifetime.

Ms. Renee hugged him. "It's going to be alright, baby, I do understand."

Sharon started to cry, too. Ms. Renee grabbed Sharon. Both kids cried for ten minutes, and after they finished, Ms. Renee wiped their faces and ran a bath with some bubbles. She put them in the bathtub together.

Deep in thought while staring at Ms. Renee, Jonathan stated this to himself: *The loving and caring touch of a mother broke down the brick wall that surrounded my heart. It opened me to feeling and helped me experience perfect love.*

"A bath will make you both feel better. You two behave, while I cook dinner. Jonathan, I'm going to wash and dry your uniform."

"Thank you."

They played in the water, and for the first time in his life Jonathan felt that someone really loved him without any conditions.

Sharon turned around and rested her small body on his chest. Jonathan grabbed her, and they sat without moving, just enjoying their young lives. Jonathan smiled and they kissed for what seemed like forever. They both put on robes that Ms. Renee had left for them.

"You two come and eat," she called from the kitchen.

"Come on, let's get some food."

Sharon held his hand as they ran down the stairs and into the dining room. Ms. Renee said a prayer, and they started to eat. She had cooked meatloaf, corn, and rice. Jonathan couldn't remember when he had ever sat down at dinner with a family. While they ate, Tiger came out of the room, acting as if nobody could see him.

Ms. Renee shouted at the dog, "Go back to your room!"

Tiger hung his head, looking gloomy, and turned around.

Sharon told her mother, "It's okay, he likes Jonathan."

"Tiger, come on, you can sit with us."

Tiger ran down the hallway toward them, then sat next to Jonathan.

"What's your last name?" Ms. Renee asked.

"Russo."

"Interesting. Do you have any brothers or sisters?"

"No brothers, but I have twenty sisters."

Ms. Renee looked shocked. "What?"

"Mama, how can someone have twenty—I mean, twenty-one—babies."

Ms. Renee smiled. "Well, Jonathan, answer the lady."

"My grandmother Aiyana, she is a Blackfoot Native American Indian. She died a few weeks ago. She told me my father kept trying on different women until he had a boy. Nina is not my sister by blood. She is Anna's child by my father's friend. Don't ask." Jonathan smiled.

"Where is your grandmother from?"

"Montana. She moved to Ohio, that's where she died. I went to Ohio with Nina over the summer to see her. I'm glad I saw her before she died. We went to Montana to have the funeral."

"Your family?" Ms. Renee asked.

"No, just me and Nina. I heard my father didn't get along with his mother."

"I'm sorry about the loss of your grandmother. How old was she?" Sharon asked.

"She was ninety-eight years old. She was a very wise woman."

Jonathan told Ms. Renee and Sharon that after the funeral, he went on a vision quest. He had left the camp alone for four days of fasting and praying. The chief of the tribe wanted him to see a vision that would explain his future. After having the vision, Jonathan returned to the village, ready to join society. He was now a warrior, as he prepared for the battles of life.

"Wow! So you really are a bad boy. Did you smoke the peace pipe?" Sharon laughed.

"No." He laughed, too. "But, yes, I am a bad boy at times."

"So, tell me about your sisters," Ms. Renee said.

"I know their names but only live with seven of them, with my father and Ms. Anna. She is not my real mother. My real mother had four kids: Lisa, Kara, Sandra, and me."

"That must be hard."

"How can that be hard?" Sharon asked. "It must be fun. I wish I had sisters."

"It's very difficult living with them. They all team up against me and beat me up. At least, I have a mini apartment and my own bathroom."

"Wait, we have a Lisa in our school," Sharon said. "She thinks she's so good looking with her light green eyes. She looks like a monster. I hope she's not your sister."

"Sharon, be nice."

"But no, Mommy, she's evil. She's always chasing boys and getting them in trouble."

Jonathan heard that description and turned white. *Shit, I hope that's not the same person*, he thought.

Ms. Renee touched his hand. "Are you okay?"

"Yes, just thinking about something."

"Well, you'd better stay away from her," Sharon said. "She's bad news."

"Okay."

"I hope they know how special you are." Ms. Renee's voice sounded so encouraging.

"No, they really don't give a shit about me."

"Mommy, he cursed."

"Sorry," Jonathan said.

"It's okay, sometimes you have to say what's on your mind."

Jonathan gave some of his meatloaf to Tiger. He and the dog became friends fast. Ms. Renee was impressed to see how quickly Tiger became attached to him.

"I don't understand that dumb dog," Ms. Renee said. "He likes Jonathan."

Sharon smiled. "He's not dumb. Tiger loves him, Mommy."

"I have two dogs," Jonathan said. "They are now my dogs. I take care of them."

"What kind?"

"Doberman pinschers."

"I hate those dogs, they're so mean," Sharon said.

"We didn't get along at first, but we now have an understanding," Jonathan said with a smirk. "One is named Thunder and the other, Lightning. My father tells stories about how these dogs have special powers and they can speak to each other. He claims they are from

Florida, descendants of Jason the Warlock. They are probably the smartest dogs in the world."

"Really, they can speak?"

"Sharon, dogs cannot speak," Ms. Renee said. "Stop being silly."

"I don't know, Ms. Renee, sometimes I think they talk to me," Jonathan said.

"The mystery is solved. That's why Tiger likes him, Mama, he's my dog man." Sharon lovingly punched him in the arm. "You are my bad boy."

"How old are you?" Ms. Renee asked. "You look so young."

"Twelve. I skipped seventh grade. I'm taking sophomore classes."

"I thought you were older," Sharon said. "So, how can you be a bad boy at twelve?"

"Okay, you two, what's the bad boy thing about?"

They answered at the same time: "Nothing." Then they laughed.

"How old are you?" Jonathan asked Sharon.

"I'm fourteen."

"See, Jonathan, you have an older woman," Ms. Renee said.

They all laughed and finished eating. Ms. Renee did the dishes, while Sharon and Jonathan completed their homework. Ms. Renee started watching television, and Sharon and Jonathan sat on the floor, playing a board game, eating marble cake, and drinking milk. It was the first home-cooked meal Jonathan had eaten in a long time.

After about an hour, Ms. Renee said, "Okay, it's time to go. Get your bag. Hey, Jonathan, don't worry. We love you." She kissed him on the lips.

"Even Tiger?"

"Yes, baby, even Tiger."

He embraced her. "I love you, too. Thank you so much. Can I come back?"

"Any time. Plus, my daughter likes you. Take care of her." She whispered, "I like you, too! You have a great future ahead of you."

"I will, you have my word, and I will take care of you, too, someday."

"I know you will, but someday you must tell me who is hurting you. Nobody cries like that and is not in a lot of pain. Believe me, I know. You have a warrior's heart."

"Someday. Someday I'll tell you, but not now, please."

"Not now, okay."

Ms. Renee drove Jonathan back to the neighborhood where he lived. He waved good-bye to them and went into the backyard to check on the dogs. Thunder and Lightning jumped around, excited to see him. Thunder sniffed his hand and smelled Tiger, then looked at Jonathan and licked his hand, as if in approval.

Jonathan went inside to fix the dogs something to eat, a nice meal of rice and chopped beef. Afterward, he took them to the woods and let them run. They all went to his room to relax.

Jonathan looked at the dogs and said, "It is going down, be on your guard."

Both dogs perked up their ears, waiting for his orders.

He turned off the television and lay in bed. That night, he knew he had to take action, or it would be a long four years. He couldn't take another beating like that—it hurt so much. However, Ms. Renee's soft touch made it feel a lot better. He fell asleep thinking about his kiss with Sharon and hoped he wouldn't get sick again by kissing these germ-filled girls. He laughed to himself and went to sleep.

Jonathan awoke around one o'clock in the morning. He waited to hear his father and the rest of the dim-witted crew leave the house. Usually, they left about one-thirty in the morning. He heard the door close and the car start.

Just like clockwork. Shit, if someone wanted to kill them, it would be easy, Jonathan thought with a smile.

He decided that he would take care of the situation in the morning, before school started. *That fucking Darrell is going to get the ass kicking of his life.*

Jonathan jumped out of bed and went down to the basement. He climbed into the crawl space under the stairs and picked up the silver 357-magnum revolver that his grandmother had given him. He loaded the gun and took approximately three hundred dollars in twenties and a roll of dimes, then hid the cash in his bedroom. He felt so happy that his grandma had given him the gun. Shooting it was easy: point and squeeze. Duke had taught him well.

Jonathan and the dogs climbed out his bedroom window, and he got on his bike. He told Thunder and Lightning to follow him. It had taken two years, but finally the dogs totally respected him. They followed his every order.

He rode his bike to Springfield Gardens Academy High School. He hid the bike in the tall shrubs and slowly walked through the cool September night back toward the house.

On the way home, the dogs went their separate ways. They went ghost. Jonathan looked for them, but they weren't around. He knew that some trouble lay ahead. Whenever they attacked, they would get very quiet about it—no barking, just biting.

An older white man came out of the bushes and asked Jonathan for a light. Jonathan told the man he didn't smoke.

The man looked him up and down and said, "I saw you. Where is your bike?"

"I don't know."

"If you don't know, then you would do."

"Do what?"

"You shouldn't be out this late, boy."

"Do what, motherfucker? You will be one sorry fuck if you touch me."

"For a young boy, you have a foul mouth. No more talking, boy. I won't be sorry, because there is nothing to be sorry about, asshole. I'm going to have some fun. Your body is going to be my playground. We have all night."

He grabbed Jonathan and pulled him close. The man had on jeans that looked as if they hadn't been washed in months and a shirt that stank of underarm odor. The stench reminded him of Lisa.

Jonathan controlled himself. He didn't want to throw up. He felt the man's heartbeat getting faster. The man had a foul odor, but Jonathan wasn't frightened. Ever since he'd gone on the vision quest, his senses had become heightened. He learned from his surroundings. He learned to use nature to protect himself.

The man had a strong grip and flipped Jonathan to the ground. He felt the man pulling on his pants. They came down, his butt was showing, and he felt the cool breeze of the night air on his legs. He lay on the warm ground with his pants down.

Jonathan didn't scream because he wasn't worried. He believed in his dogs. This was their first test together.

"Please don't hurt me," he said quietly.

The man said, "This young ass belongs to me. You're not fighting me off, so I guess you want it, right?"

"Let me go!" Jonathan kicked at the man.

"That's it. I like it when they fight."

Jonathan thought that this fucker had done this shit before. "You fuck!"

Jonathan saw Thunder's eyes between the shrubs.

"I'm not the fuck, but I'm going to fuck that young tight sweet ass."

The man had his foot on the midsection of Jonathan's back, so he couldn't move. Then he felt the pressure lift off him. He turned around and saw the man drop his pants.

Jonathan thought to himself, *There is no way in this lifetime this is going have a good ending.*

Just as the man tugged down his pants, Jonathan tried to reach for his gun. His hand got stuck, because the man's foot pressed on his back.

Thunder jumped out of the bushes onto the man's chest. The dog's momentum knocked the man to the ground, and Thunder grabbed his neck but didn't bite down yet.

The man squealed and pleaded for the dog to let him go. Lightning jumped on the man and waited for Jonathan to get up. Jonathan rose to his feet and watched his dogs hold the man down.

The man screamed and cried. "Please, no, I'm so sorry. I'll be good, please, I will never do this again."

The dogs didn't take their eyes off Jonathan. He walked over to the man lying on the ground and looked at him. He calmly said, "Fuck you."

"No, please, don't do this, you'll go to jail. I'm a police officer."

"Nice. Then you will be a dead cop. I should put a bullet in your fucked head."

"You can't kill a cop."

"Really. Why not?"

"You'll die in jail," the man said. "I can help you."

"You're going to die *tonight* for every little boy you assaulted."

Lightning bit into the man's mouth until he couldn't speak anymore. She pulled his lip and tore it off.

Thunder chomped down harder on the man's neck until blood squirted out of his veins. While Lightning ripped at the man's mouth, Jonathan zipped up his pants and then joined in by kicking the man.

This went on for about ten minutes, until the man had stopped moving. There was blood all over the street and on Jonathan's shoes.

"I hoped you suffered," Jonathan said.

The man moved a little. "Why? I don't want to die."

"We don't get what we want all the time."

"Have mercy."

Jonathan directed his dogs to kill the man, then kicked him in the head. The dogs each grabbed one side of the man's neck and pulled, until Thunder jerked some skin off the man's body. Lightning fell back as she ripped off a section of the man's neck.

He stopped moving. Jonathan gave him one last kick and watched the man bleed out.

When it was over, Thunder and Lightning walked proudly, side by side, with their new leader, the new alpha. Back at the house, he cleaned them off.

Jonathan sat on the bed. He felt alone. He couldn't be sure how he felt about taking someone's life. His dogs and his hands had killed a man.

If this was going to be his life, then acceptance had to happen tonight. No remorse. He could either keep hurting or try to live the best he could. He was smart enough to know that people didn't give a shit about him. Therefore, if someone had to die at his hands, then so be it.

He realized that he felt no guilt. He did not cry. Furthermore, he wasn't cold and withdrawn. He felt more of a sense of satisfaction that this man would never touch anybody again.

FIVE

The alarm clock went off at 6 a.m. on Wednesday morning. It was the second day of school. Jonathan had a big day ahead of him and felt nervous while getting dressed. He put on his black pants and a white shirt, the school uniform for first-year students. When he went to the kitchen to get some juice, he saw his father and Judy.

"Good morning, Judy."

"What the fuck is so good about it?" Judy put her hands on her hips and said, "I heard you got your ass kicked. I thought you were some kind of warrior."

"I fell in the gym." Jonathan wondered how she knew, but he couldn't be bothered explaining it to her.

"Who got their ass kicked?" his father yelled from the other room.

"Your dumb-ass son," Judy said.

Frankie J and Judy laughed.

"Leave him alone," Nina said. "Pick on someone else."

"What's up with you?" Judy turned and looked at Nina. "Are you protecting your man? You both disgust me."

"Judy, you really get on my nerves," Nina said.

"Keep it up, bitch."

"Go fuck yourself."

"Okay, cut the shit," Frankie J said. "Come over here, boy. What happened to you yesterday?"

Jonathan didn't need any further confrontations, because he had to stay focused. He walked over to his father and explained how he fell running in gym. He looked over to see Anna sleeping on the floor. No doubt, she'd had her share of liquor and drugs last night. Tommy and Rico were playing cards, as his other sisters talked with one another. Jonathan took a good look at Tommy, and he could see a resemblance to Nina.

He thought, *This is a fucked-up family.*

"He's a liar!" Judy shouted.

"Are you lying to me, boy?"

Jonathan didn't want to look like he was trying to deceive his father, so he said, "No," without changing his facial expression.

"Call me if you need me to come to your school."

"Okay, I have to go."

"Give your dad a hug."

Jonathan didn't like his father, especially when he was drunk. That's when his father always acted as if they were the best of friends.

Jonathan turned his attention to a report on the TV morning news about the death of a police officer.

"A man was viciously mauled in the Springfield Gardens area, police said. He was mauled by unknown animals on one hundred and thirty-fifth road about one-thirty Wednesday morning, police officers said. He lived nearby and was dead at the scene. It was not immediately clear what caused the animals to attack. Furthermore, the reporter noted that his pants were down and his private parts were exposed. Detective Victor Greenwood was a fifteen-year veteran with the New York City Police Department. The investigation continues," the reporter said.

"Judy, was this your work last night?" his father joked.

Judy entered the living room and looked at the TV screen, to see a man lying on the ground. "No, not me."

Frankie J winked at Judy. She walked back to the kitchen. Jonathan knew that Judy didn't have the heart to kill, but he promised himself that he would never underestimate a woman.

When Jonathan returned to the kitchen, Judy was washing dishes. *One second, she's a gangster and the next a homemaker*, he thought.

"I know you're lying," Judy said.

"Whatever!"

He didn't have time for Judy today, so he didn't pay her any attention. She was just another low-class skank with a gun.

He went to his bedroom and pulled the Smith and Wesson .357 magnum from under the bed, then tucked it in his waistband. He stuffed some cash in his pocket and put a pair of gloves, a roll of dimes, and a water gun in his school bag. On his way out the door, Nina called to him.

"Jonathan, come here, baby. Have a good day at school. I love you."

"Thanks."

"What the fuck?" Judy asked. "Did you two bond in Montana?"

Nina gave Judy a dirty look. "Just go," she said, hurrying Jonathan out the door.

Jonathan moved closer to Nina and whispered, "I love you, too."

He went to the back yard to see the dogs.

"See you soon, off to war." They didn't move; they just sat there. Jonathan opened the gate to the dogs' pen and left it ajar.

On his way to school, he walked with the confidence and nonchalance of a skilled killer, to hide his extreme nervousness. Jonathan was entering the point of no return. If he killed Darrell or one of the gang members, it would be over for him—maybe jail time.

He didn't take the usual road to school, because he observed police officers in the neighborhood. They were out in force after last night's butchery of one of their own. Jonathan gave the matter some thought and then told himself, *Fuck that, man.*

He could see the clock tower on the school as he got closer. Turning his head, he glimpsed Sharon. He walked over and kissed her on the lips. "You look so nice today."

"Thanks," Sharon said.

"Hey, I was thinking about you last night."

"Me, too!"

"Listen, take my bag and go across the street. I'll see you around fourth period."

"Where're you going?" She pulled Jonathan toward her. "Please come with me. Don't fight again. It's not worth it. They'll hurt you."

"I know," he said, clenching his fists. "Don't worry, I'm not going to let those white boys be the law around here. Those bullies stop today! I would rather die than submit to their will."

She frowned. "Look! I don't want you to get injured." She grabbed his arm and held him firmly.

He pulled his arm away and pointed a finger in her face. "Just do what I ask."

Sharon reluctantly walked across the street, turning her head occasionally. Jonathan could see sadness in her eyes. He realized that she actually cared about him. He also understood that if he became seriously wounded, he would break her heart and lose his football scholarship.

Jonathan put the roll of dimes in the right glove and put it on. He adjusted his glove, then walked up to Darrell.

"Yo, look who's back in the motherfucking house," one of the gang members said.

"You're going to pay for what you did to my boy Carl," Darrell said.

"I hope the fucker dies," Jonathan said.

"If he dies, you die," promised Darrell.

"You're to blame if he dies," Jonathan said. "Don't you know that you never leave a man behind on the battlefield?"

"What did you say to me?" Darrell asked.

Jonathan shook his head. "Dumb fuck."

"Fuck that jerk up, kick his ass," another gang member said. "Little fuck face, you wanna fight me?"

Jonathan squared off with Darrell, but Darrell's boys shoved him from behind, and he fell forward to the ground. They kicked and punched him, and Jonathan could taste blood in his mouth. The longer he lay on the ground, the more they walloped him. He tried to get control of the situation by swinging his arms as fast as he could, but it didn't help. There were too many of them. He heard the crowd in the background, yelling for the gang to kill him.

Five minutes into the fight, Jonathan heard a loud bark.

They're here, he thought. He thanked God, because the beating he was taking hurt really bad.

Thunder grabbed one of the boys, and he fell to the ground.

Jonathan was able to free himself. Lightning got another boy. Many of the others ran away. Some were too afraid to move. Jonathan jumped up and saw Darrell looking at the dogs. He shouted at his gang not to run.

When Darrell turned his attention to the others, it gave Jonathan a brief tactical advantage. He attacked by surprise, flipping Darrell to the ground, with his left hand around Darrell's neck, choking him. With his right hand, he repeatedly hit Darrell in the face.

Jonathan wanted to destroy Darrell to ensure that the bully would never attack him again. He kept punching Darrell, who tried to block and cover his face. But Jonathan's power and speed, along with the roll of dimes in his glove, made for a very effective weapon. He grabbed Darrell's neck again and choked him.

He watched as Darrell's face turned from red to blue. Darrell tried to talk, but no sound came out. He mouthed the words "Please stop."

Jonathan looked around and saw that the dogs had everything under control. He let go of Darrell's neck and pulled out his gun, then stuck the pistol in Darrell's face.

"Open up, bitch."

"No. Please. No!"

"Not a request, not a fucking request," Jonathan said, shaking his gun in Darrell's face. "I'm not going to ask you again."

Jonathan looked at Darrell and could see fear in his eyes.

Jonathan got so excited, he cocked the pistol and put the gun on Darrell's lips. Yet he was very careful to block the view of the gun so that nobody could see it. "I want to kill you so bad, I think I could pee my pants."

Jonathan pushed the gun farther into Darrell's mouth. "If you ever fuck with me again or anyone I'm with, I will kill everyone in your fucking family. Tell me you understand."

Tears flowed out of Darrell's eyes. His face was bloody, and he shook his head yes.

"Say it."

"Yes, I'm sorry. Please stop."

Jonathan uncocked the gun, because he figured Darrell had had enough and he'd had enough. No more fighting for now. He'd made his point.

A large crowd of students had gathered. Jonathan put the gun back in his pants and walked over to the two people the dogs held down. He told Thunder and Lightning to go home. The dogs ran down the street. Jonathan kicked one boy in the face several times and stomped on the other boy's chest.

Jonathan climbed the fence and found the bike he'd left the night before. He rode back to the house.

There, he changed his school uniform, then hid the bloody gloves and the gun in the dogs' pen. He fixed some food for the dogs and made his way back to school. He entered through the back door, because he saw the police at the front entrance. He arrived at his fourth-period class late.

As he entered the classroom, the music teacher said, "Mr. Russo, I don't know what kind of school you came from before you got here, but I do not tolerate lateness." The teacher paused and asked, "Do you understand?"

"Okay, boss, it won't happen again."

"See that it doesn't. Now go and find a seat."

Jonathan looked around the class and walked over to sit beside Sharon.

Sharon whispered, "You're some kind of bad-ass boy."

Jonathan smiled.

"So the word is that they're going to come after you. Watch your back. It's going to get worse. Nobody ever fought back with them."

Jonathan didn't know much about being a "leader" or a "bad boy," but he knew those guys weren't going to give him a pass. They would either call the police or handle the situation themselves. And because they were punks and wouldn't want to take this any further, he told himself, *Expect the police.*

He reached over and kissed Sharon on the cheek. "Hey, you, I told you it would be okay. Just hang in there with me."

If they come at me again, he thought, *I'll kill them all, because I now believe that to defend myself from any person or persons who have injured me and tried to cause me bodily harm, it's not wrong to use any weapon available. The whole purpose of this is to ensure that they think twice before foolishly attacking me again.* He smiled.

The class had been set up auditorium-style. As the teacher talked about music theory, Jonathan looked around and saw half of the kids sleeping. The study and notation of music and identifying patterns and structures in composers' techniques were not the most interesting topics in the world. They numbed the brain, if you didn't care about then.

Jonathan started thinking about what to say if he were called to the principal's office. He'd covered his tracks. He had concealed the gun under the dogs' house. Then he'd put some meat in the bloody gloves and let the dogs deal with them, knowing Thunder and Lightning would fight over the gloves all day. Jonathan felt thrilled that he'd gotten his point across.

After a few moments of silence, he heard footsteps. The door opened. Everyone in the class looked shocked to see eight police officers, along with the principal, the vice principal, and the football coach.

"Russo, stand up," the principal said.

One police officer yelled out, "Slowly!"

Jonathan looked around the classroom and said, "Go fly a kite!"

"Son, don't make this any worse for yourself," the older cop said. "Just stand up, put your hands up, and walk toward us."

"Whatever! You're picking on me 'cause I'm black."

Jonathan turned, looked at Sharon, and winked. "Hey, don't worry, I'll be back by lunch. Save me a seat!" he yelled.

He walked toward the officers with his middle finger extended.

The cops pushed Jonathan against the wall and searched him, then handcuffed him. The younger police officer picked up Jonathan's bag and looked inside. He found the gun and held it up.

"It's just a water gun," the cop said.

The class broke into laughter.

"Knock it off," the principal said. "Continue with your class."

"Dumb ass," Jonathan said, looking at the cop.

Jonathan didn't have any real feeling about cops. They'd never bothered him, but he didn't think they were too smart.

While they were in the principal's office, he waited for them to finish talking with one another.

"Do you have a gun?" the older white cop asked.

"Just the water gun. Why?"

"Look, boy!"

Jonathan was not overly shocked by what the police officer had said. He responded, "You're a real jerk. Take these cuffs off me."

"Those boys you beat up will press charges, and you'll go to jail."

"No, I won't."

"If they said you had a gun, then you had a gun," the older white cop said. "I can't wait to get you to the station."

"Just because they're white, they think they can get away with crimes," Jonathan said. "I want my father."

"You don't get what you want," the cop said.

"Okay, we'll see when he gets here." Deep down, Jonathan knew it was a big mistake to call his father, but he needed him.

"You have a bad attitude, little boy," said the vice principal. "You will never play football at this school."

After about twenty minutes, Jonathan's father walked in, accompanied by Judy, Tommy, and Rico. Jonathan's father walked over to the principal.

"Why's my son in handcuffs?"

Tommy took out his detective's shield and flashed it to the other police officers.

"You heard the man. Take that boy out of those handcuffs now!"

"Somebody needs to explain to me what he did to warrant this many police officers here," his father said.

The principal said, "Mr. Russo, your son beat up three upstanding students, and they are in the hospital now."

His father laughed. "My boy, he's only four feet tall. Who can he beat up? I think this matter is settled!"

"Son, tell your father what happened," the principal said.

"We were boxing for fun, and nobody got hurt. I went back home to change my uniform 'cause it got dirty. I don't know what happened after I left."

"Okay, I've heard enough," the principal said. "Come on, boy, go to class."

Jonathan got up, turned around, and gave them the middle finger.

His father scowled at him. "We will talk about this when you get home."

Jonathan, his father, and their entourage walked out of the office.

Judy grabbed Jonathan by the neck. "I'm going to kill you when you get in tonight."

Jonathan stared at Judy and said, "Go fuck yourself."

He walked to the lunchroom. When he entered the cafeteria's double doors, all of the students became silent. Sharon waved for him to come over. The students stared at him, then began clapping. Jonathan presidentially raised both arms with his palms outward, index and middle fingers extended, as he flashed the peace sign. It was a great victory.

He kissed Sharon on the lips, and everyone in the lunchroom cheered louder. Sharon explained that Darrell and his crew had terrorized the students for the last four years, and he was the first person to successfully stand up to them. Darrell had put many kids in the hospital or made them transfer to a new school, especially the black students.

After school, Jonathan put his arm around Sharon's waist, and they slowly walked to her house.

Tyrone and his brother Trey pulled up alongside them. There were five cars full of guys who looked like they were ready for war.

Trey got out of the car. "I heard there was trouble. You good?" Trey asked.

"Yeah."

"Let me know if you need help," Trey said.

"I got this," Jonathan said.

"Later," Tyrone said, while he looked Sharon up and down.

They drove away. Jonathan wasn't going to ask for a favor. He knew Trey would never let him pay it back. Jonathan would always owe him. Trey would keep coming back. Enough was never enough with Trey. Plus, Jonathan didn't need them; he had it handled.

"Who was that?" Sharon asked.

"Nobody good. Come, let's go to your house.

"That's it. You kick ass and then you dismiss me?"

"What are you talking about?"

"Nothing!"

Jonathan stopped and hugged Sharon. "Listen, I got you, don't ask so many questions. We'll be okay."

"Sure, but one day will you tell me who you really are?"

They went to her room, and she started kissing him all over. It's not that he didn't like it, but his body was sore. Yet it was nothing a little pussy couldn't help. After they finished, they did their homework. He felt happy to see Ms. Renee again. She cooked dinner, and they ate.

"I hate to eat and run, but I need to deal with something."

"Be careful and call me later."

Jonathan kissed Sharon and hugged Ms. Renee.

He took a slow walk back to the house, no need to rush. He knew his father and his sister would give him a violent beating. It was going to be a long night. Only a bullet to his head would stop the beating that was in store for him. He could try to get the jump on them and kill them all, but he knew he would be dead before he got one shot off.

When he arrived home, his sisters were sitting in the living room, along with his father, Tommy, Judy, Rico, and Anna, his stepmother.

"Did you think you were going to get away with that shit?" Judy asked.

"I'm sorry," Jonathan said.

"Fuck sorry."

"What going on?" Jonathan asked.

"Tell us what happened in school and why you find it necessary to humiliate this family," his father said.

"Like I said earlier, I don't know what happened."

"I'm going kick your ass until next week, boy. Now tell us what you did."

Jonathan knew that no matter what he said, it wouldn't go well.

"But those boys were bothering me. I didn't do anything wrong."

"Being born, that's what you did wrong," Anna said.

"You know what? Do what you're going to do," Jonathan said. "I don't care."

"You're truly a little asshole, and I'm going to kill you!" Judy yelled.

"See, the problem is, you think I care." Jonathan dropped his school bag. "You know what? As far as I'm concerned, Judy, you can suck my fucking dick. Just thinking about it a little further, all you fuckers could line up and suck my dick, too! Dumb bitches!"

Frankie J laughed, and Judy said, "Frankie, don't encourage him."

"That's some funny shit," Frankie said.

"You will never embarrass this family again," Judy said.

Jonathan looked at his father for help, but Frankie J hung his head. Judy grabbed Jonathan by the neck and threw him to the floor. The sisters joined in and started punching him. Judy pounded on his leg, and normally Jonathan wouldn't have said anything, but it was too much pain. The more they kicked him, the louder he called Nina.

"Help me, Nina! Help me, Nina!"

"Leave him alone!" Nina shouted. "He's just a little boy! Leave him alone!"

Judy got up off Jonathan and turned her attention to Nina. "This is the last time you ever talk back to me."

As Judy approached Nina, Nina jumped off the chair and swung at Judy. But Judy was just too strong for her. Judy tossed her and threw her around like a toy doll. Judy had Nina on the ground and kicked her in the face.

Jonathan punched Gail in the chest, and when she moved off him, he hit her again.

He heard Anna say, "Kill the boy."

All of his sisters jumped him. He managed to fight his way out and got up to help Nina. Judy picked Nina up and slammed her to the ground again. On her way down, she hit her head against the coffee table. All hell broke loose in the living room. Jonathan couldn't take it anymore and started swinging back, punching his sisters. He spun around and grabbed Judy to get her off Nina. When he looked up, Tommy was right on top of him.

"Enough!" Rico yelled.

Jonathan's father said, "I will tell you when it's enough."

Tommy looked at Frankie J and shook his head. Frankie J told everyone to stop, and just like that, everyone stopped. Jonathan picked up a knife he saw on the floor and went after Judy.

Tommy saw him and knocked him to the floor before he could cut Judy. Tommy told everyone to calm down. Jonathan got up off the floor and went to Nina. Her nose was bleeding.

Tommy took both of them to Jonathan's part of the house. He brought Jonathan into the bathroom and closed the door.

"Are we okay?"

"It's not fair, Tommy. No one should be treated like this. It's not fair."

"I know, but sometimes you do things that you really don't want to do. Sometimes life is just not fair. Again, are we okay?"

"Tommy, you never have to worry about anything. I would rather cut my own throat than say anything about you. Yes, we're okay."

Because of the beating and because Tommy really hadn't intervened, he'd been worried that Jonathan would try to save his own skin and tell Frankie J that Tommy and Rico were screwing each other. But Jonathan knew he had a good thing, and all he had to do was keep his mouth shut.

After Tommy and Rico left the room, Nina lay in Jonathan's bed, crying. In the bathroom, Jonathan ran a tub full of water and added bubble bath. He climbed into the tub and relaxed. Nina came in to see what he was doing. She took off her clothes and got into the tub with him, then leaned on his chest and sobbed.

SIX

The day before Thanksgiving, Jonathan went to Sharon's house. As they sat in the living room watching college football on TV, she fell asleep on his lap. She was suffering from bad menstrual cramps. In the kitchen, Nina and Ms. Renee cooked, drank wine, and talked about men. Jonathan heard them laughing and joking about things they'd done in the past.

Jonathan felt concerned about Nina. Lately, she seemed distracted. She had lost weight and had gone missing for a few days at a time. The dogs, Thunder, Lightning, and Tiger, were in the backyard, playing tug-of-war.

The doorbell rang, and Tiger started barking. Ms. Renee went to the window see who was there.

"Oh, no!" she said, backing away.

"What's the matter, Ms. Renee?" Jonathan asked.

"Sharon, get up. Get up now! It's your father."

"What? Why? Mommy?"

Nina walked into the room, "What's up?"

"I don't know," Jonathan said.

Sharon's father had been in Downstate Correctional Facility in Fishkill, New York. The charge was first-degree rape; he'd gotten fifteen years but after five years was out. He had raped his daughter Sharon and put her in the hospital for seven days with a bruised cervix. He had been released from prison that day.

Sharon got up and stared at the door, frozen. Ms. Renee, Nina, and Jonathan stood in the living room without moving.

"Evil lives inside of me," Sharon cried, pointing her finger at her chest.

"What?" Jonathan asked.

"Open the door, Renee! I hear you in there!" James shouted.

"No, Mommy, please, please no." Sharon started to weep.

Renee opened the door, and James pushed his way into the house. He was over six feet tall and well built. He looked around the room, then opened his arms and said, "No hug for Daddy?"

"James, you can't stay here."

"This is my house, bitch. I can do whatever the fuck I want, so fix me a drink."

He turned to his daughter. "Sharon, my baby, come here."

Sharon didn't respond but only stared blankly at James. When she started to move, Jonathan stopped her. James looked at Jonathan with anger, then glanced at Nina.

"I want to die," Sharon said, pointing at her father. "He planted a seed in my body to remind me that he would always be inside of me."

Jonathan noticed blood running down her leg.

"My daddy fucked me, and now I bleed. I'm dying."

Blood dripped from her leg onto the rug. James walked toward Sharon, and Ms. Renee stepped between them.

"Leave her."

"What the fuck did you do to her?" Jonathan said.

"Yo, I'll kick your ass, so mind your fucking business."

Nina walked over to Jonathan and Sharon and protectively hugged them. Jonathan thought he could get two shots off before James knew what hit him. He started to reach for his gun, then Sharon shook off Nina's hug and moved toward her father. She yanked up her dress, reached into her panties, pulled out her tampon, and dropped it on the floor. Everyone watched in disbelief.

"My daddy fucked me, and now I bleed," she said again. "You bastard, you. You're the one who did this shit to me."

Jonathan froze, leaving his weapon concealed.

Sharon picked up the tampon and rubbed in her father's face. "This blood is for you, Daddy!"

James slapped Sharon with so much force, she fell to the floor.

"You crazy bitch," he said.

Jonathan actually thought the same thing, but he could understand a person losing control. Ms. Renee pushed James, but he didn't flinch. He kicked her in the chest.

Nina tried to hold Jonathan back, but he ran over to James and jumped up to hit him in the face. James lifted Jonathan off his feet and flung him against the wall.

James grabbed Ms. Renee and choked her, demanding money. He tried kissing her on the lips.

Furious, Jonathan told him to get off her. James walked over to Jonathan, picked him up again, and threw him onto the couch. Nina helped Ms. Renee off the floor, and they both grabbed Sharon.

Jonathan found himself trying to decide whether to kill James or murder everyone in the house. He wasn't thinking logically. His whole reason for killing James was to protect Sharon and Ms. Renee, but then if he did commit murder in front of them, they'd be witnesses and might turn him in to the cops. Yet if he killed them, he would no longer need to protect them, so he'd have no motive for killing James. His mind ran in circles like a snake biting its tail. He had to think fast. Did everyone in this room have to die? He tried to control his anger, but it had taken hold of him.

Jonathan finally calmed down and decided to negotiate with James. He realized that money would help get James out of the house.

"Okay," he yelled. "Stop! Let's take a minute."

The room got quiet, with the exception of Sharon, still crying.

"What?" James said.

"Let's make a deal. It's about money."

"What the fuck does a little boy like you knows about money?"

"Don't worry about it. I can give you five thousand now and five tomorrow. But you can't stay here."

James's face softened. "I'm listening."

Jonathan pulled the cash out of his pocket. James's eyes widened.

From the corner of his eye, Jonathan saw Lightning, who had pushed through the open front door. "I'll give you the money, and you don't come back tonight. Come back tomorrow around this time, and I'll give you the rest. Deal?"

"Deal, hell yeah, motherfucker. Now that's what's up. Give me the money."

"No, not yet. We're going to make the change in the park. So let's go."

"Fuck that shit! Give me my money now, motherfucker."

Lightning came into full view of James and barked furiously at him.

James backed off a little. "Okay, fine. Let's go. I see you bitches later."

"Only in your fucking nightmare," Jonathan said. He grabbed his coat and told his ladies he would be back in an hour. Nina told him to be careful. Jonathan called Thunder from the back.

"That's a big dog."

"He will slaughter you if you try to fuck with me again."

"Fuck them."

"Jonathan, don't go," Ms. Renee said.

"I'll be fine."

While Jonathan, James, Lightning, and Tiger walked to the park, James kept talking about how many people he'd killed, how much drugs he'd sold, and all of the things he'd done in the streets. He talked about his time in prison and how he was the king.

Jonathan was thinking that James had spent the last five years getting fucked up the ass and crying for his mother. He just needed to shut up. Jonathan knew he had to kill James. A person like that would always keep coming back.

In the park, they took the path to the lake. Jonathan knew that Thunder was not far away.

"Let's do this here," Jonathan said.

"You think you're doing the right thing?"

"For Renee and Sharon, I'd do anything for them."

"Whatever, fuck those bitches. Give me my money."

James clutched Jonathan's arm with one hand and, with the other, grabbed his neck. Thunder jumped out of the bushes and seized James's arm. Lightning pulled him to the ground and held him there.

"What the fuck?" he screamed.

"You fuck. Did you believe I was going to give you money? Shit, you're one fucked-up dumb-ass person."

Jonathan pulled out his gun and put the silencer on. He saw fear in James's eyes, as he started to beg for his life.

Jonathan laughed at him. "Some guys are fake and talk about how they put in work by bragging about shit to improve their image. They put it in their songs, movies, videos, and talk about the bodies they have on them. Nevertheless, it's all counterfeit. Fake-ass like you, James, you never put any real work in. You can tell bitch because when they're in a life-or-death situation, they cry like a little bitch. Just like you, James."

"Fuck you. I have seen killers, and I can look into your eyes and tell that you're no killer."

"Look again, bitch, tell me if I have fear in my eyes. This is for Sharon and Renee."

Jonathan remembered his training with Duke. Aim and squeeze the trigger, but he thought that *pull* sounded better. *Who cares? The result is still the same*, Jonathan thought. Duke told him that techniques are important; the name is not.

"I don't want to die," James pleaded.

Jonathan shot James in the heart and watched him take his last breath.

He shot James through the heart again and then one time in head. Duke had told him two in the heart and one in the head. He checked the man's pulse to make sure James was dead and pushed the body into the deep bushes before leaving Locust Manor Park.

Breathing in the cool air of the autumn night, Jonathan and the dogs imperiously walked back to Sharon's house. He only had Sharon on his mind. He had a key, and when he opened the door, Ms. Renee and Nina stood there to meet him.

"Are you okay?" Nina asked, hugging him.

"I'm well. He's not coming back." He hugged Ms. Renee. "Where is she?"

Nina pointed upstairs. Jonathan went up to Sharon's bedroom. She lay in bed, resting.

"Hey."

Jonathan took off his coat and shoes and got into bed with her. Watching her, he held her as tight as he could, while waiting for her to talk first. After a few minutes, she broke the silence.

"I'm sorry."

Jonathan thought, *it would be impossible to know how someone feels, with every negative emotion they experience. These conversations with people and how they express their feelings I may not fully understand; however, I can truly appreciate their pain.*

"You scared me," Jonathan said. "I've seen a lot in my life but never that. Do you want to kill yourself?"

"Yes, sometimes I think about it. Do you hate me?"

"No, but I'm very worried about you. At some point, you have to get some help. I may be young, but in my house I've lived a lifetime. Suicide will free your body from life, but it will imprison your soul to internal damnation."

"Wow! I'm not crazy. I don't need to go to the nut house," Sharon objected. "I couldn't take it, seeing him again. I thought I would be long gone before he got out of prison."

"What did you mean, he planted a seed in your body?"

"He took something from me."

Jonathan told her what had happened two years earlier with Lisa. He said he also felt that his innocence was stolen from him. How he wished he'd never taken that route to school that day! He hated her for what she'd done to him.

"I never thought there would come a time in my life when my innocence would be so abruptly taken away, and I'd want to die. But not anymore—I want to live," Jonathan declared.

"Yes, Mr. Bad Boy, I feel the same way. I hope my father overdoses on drugs tonight. I hope he dies. But it's funny, I still love him."

"Do you mean that? Because he will never come back, so don't worry anymore."

"Yes. I hate him and love him at the same time. What do you mean, he's not coming back?"

"He got what I think he deserved." Jonathan kissed her. "You shouldn't worry about it. Just go on with your life. Go to sleep."

He waited until she fell asleep and left her room. He and Nina kissed Ms. Renee good night.

"Do you think he's coming back?"

"I'm confident he will never bother you again," Jonathan said.

Thunder and Lightning followed Nina and Jonathan down the street. Nina suggested that they not go home right then. She didn't feel like going back to the house, because of what had happened to Sharon. She wanted to go someplace and just talk awhile. They decided on Montbellier Park.

At the park, Nina rolled a joint from the weed Jonathan had gotten from Tyrone. She took a bottle of Wild Irish Rose wine out of her bag. It was around seven o'clock in the evening, with a cold wind blowing. Jonathan couldn't remember when he'd had a family dinner, but he knew that when he got older, it would be better. It was the day before Thanksgiving, and they talked and got drunk from the cheap wine, while Thunder and Lightning ran and played on the football field. They came to terms with a critical fact: it was mandatory that they stay away from Judy.

"What happened with James?"

He shrugged. "It's taken care of, and that's really all you need to know."

"So you're not going to tell me."

"Yes, I will someday. It's not that important really, so don't worry about it. I had to make sure you, Renee, and Sharon were safe."

"You know, some days you talk like a little boy who's not sure of himself and then other days you sound like a grown man in charge. Okay, fine, but am I safe?"

He looked at her and said, "Trixie."

"You haven't called me that in a while."

"I . . .," He paused. "Nothing. I got the feeling you didn't like it."

"I don't," she said. "You know that your girlfriend is crazy as hell. I never have seen any shit like that. If this is long term, then you might have a problem."

"I know. I don't think it will be long term, but I do like her a lot. We shall see."

Jonathan asked Nina to move into his side of the house, which had three rooms: a bathroom with a shower and a bathtub, a bedroom with a king-size bed, and a walk-in closet. There was more than enough space for both of them. His area of the house was a mini apartment that, if it had been situated in a different way, could probably hold at least four to six people. He also had a refrigerator and a mini oven. Nina felt happy that she would be with Jonathan, out of the way of her sisters, and wouldn't have to participate in their illegal activities anymore.

"I do love you," Nina said, "and I'm sorry for all the beatings I helped them give you."

"Thanks. I love you, too."

"Hey, I know, let's seal this with a kiss," Nina said.

"Stop playing. I don't like to kiss."

"That's because you don't know how." Nina started to tickle him, and he laughed.

"Okay."

"Kiss me."

Jonathan knew they were not bound by blood, so why not? They both were drunk anyway. They looked at each other, and without hesitation, he kissed her. Nina pulled away and said, "I know you don't kiss your girlfriend this way."

"What?"

"You are too hard, too rough. Let me show you. It should be slow. Kissing is like dancing to a slow song. You know how to dance, right?"

Nina showed Jonathan how to kiss, and he lost control of his feelings because it felt so good. It made him excited, and whenever he got sexually excited, his mouth got wet. His saliva glands worked overtime.

"And that's how you kiss a girl. Don't forget it." Nina wiped her mouth and said, "That's a lot of kissing juice."

"What?"

"I'm going to teach you how to control yourself when you're kissing a girl. You don't have to produce some much spit."

When the kissing lesson was over, Jonathan was speechless. He just stared at Nina. They finished the wine, he called the dogs, and they exited the park. They held hands walking back to the house and didn't say a word.

SEVEN

I t had been three years since Jonathan had shot and killed Sharon's father, James. He had never heard any news reports about that incident, and Sharon didn't talk about it. Since that day, Jonathan and Sharon had become inseparable. At times, he'd wanted to tell her what had happened, but he decided against it. One thing he knew was that people cannot be loyal. They will tell on you in a minute, if you don't dance to their beat.

Every so often, he wondered why he didn't feel guilty or have any remorse for the two people who had died because of him. Maybe it was a character defect, because he realized that he felt superior in his mind. He'd never thought of himself as an arrogant person, but he had to remind himself that he didn't want to end up like his father.

Nina and Ms. Renee became friends. Jonathan thought about how far he had come in life, despite the many obstacles he'd faced every day. He still had not grown much bigger. Because he was smart, he'd skipped some classes. At the age of fifteen, he was taking senor classes at the Springfield Gardens Preparatory High School. It looked as if he would graduate when he turned sixteen. His football career was going well. He was chosen as the Most Valuable Player in the State of New York.

Spring break rolled around, and Jonathan hadn't seen Nina in two days. He felt concerned and didn't know where to look. Sitting on his bed, he told himself that he would wait two more hours. After that, he would go look for her. He wasn't sure what to do. He decided that if she were not back, he would tell Ms. Renee.

Jonathan heard a knock on the back door. He saw Nina through the window. She didn't look well. Her beautiful skin was pale. When he opened the door, she fell into his arms.

"Where were you?"

"You don't want to know. Do you have any money?

"For what?"

"I'm sorry. I am so sorry." Her expression turned into a frown.

"You had better tell me what's going on. I'm not playing, Nina."

Nina started to cry, and she fell to her knees. Jonathan saw bruises on her neck and legs.

"Please, I need money."

"Tell me something."

"I'm scared to tell you, John John."

"Why?"

Jonathan helped her off the floor and walked her to the bathroom. He ran the bath water, while she sat in the chair and cried. She took off her sweaty, dirty jeans and top.

"I thought we got past that. You should be able to tell me anything so I can help you."

"I'm so sorry," she said again.

"What's wrong?"

"I'm in trouble."

"Tell me what's wrong. I need to know what's up with you. I don't like this."

"I know," she said. "I don't want you to get hurt, so I don't want to bother you."

"You don't want to bother me? Then why do I feel so fucking bothered? If it involves you, it involves me. Tell me what the fuck is going."

"I owe Trey some money."

"What the fuck are you doing with Trey? Did he beat you?"

Nina put her head between her legs and said, "Yes."

She told Jonathan she had been smoking crack cocaine, and when she ran out of money, she'd gotten drugs on credit. She owed Trey

$300. If she didn't have the money by that night, it would go up to $400.

Jonathan hugged her and reassured her that everything would be okay. He went outside to get Thunder and Lightning and brought them into the bedroom. Nina had just gotten out of the bathtub and was drying off. Jonathan could see more cuts and bruises on her body.

He told her not to leave the room under any circumstances. He turned on the television and gave her a Valium, so that she could come down off her high. He ordered the dogs to stand watch. Thunder moved toward Jonathan, but he told the dog that he had to go alone.

Jonathan didn't like Trey or his brother Tyrone. They were trouble. He went to his cash supply and grabbed $20,000. He had a lot of money because Tommy and Rico kept giving it to him. He knew they didn't have to, but he took it anyway. He'd saved enough money to pay for college, if he didn't get a full scholarship. There had to be about $80,000 in the safe.

He piled the cash into four stacks, with $5,000 in each. He figured $20,000 was enough. He retrieved his Glock 29 and three extra clips. *Forty rounds should be plenty*, he thought.

Nina lay on the bed, crying.

Jonathan walked over and whispered in her ear, "I'm sorry I yelled at you. I want you to stay in the room. Don't leave, okay?"

"Okay," she said. "What are you going to do?"

"I'm going to take of this mess. Don't leave this room and get some rest. Thunder and Lightning will protect you."

"Please be careful. Did anyone know I was missing?"

"No, I didn't tell."

Jonathan grabbed his backpack, went outside, and got his bike. He knew Trey's crew, Lil' Trouble Makers. Jonathan had been in that crew, but he'd gotten out before it turned into a criminal enterprise. They always hung out on Merrick and 215th Street.

It was warm for the month of April, and Jonathan was on a mission. He wished he had his dogs, but sometimes it was necessary to do without help. He saw his old friend Ray, who was now a low-level drug dealer for Lil' Trouble Makers.

"Yo, Jonathan, what's up, my son?"

"Nothing." They gave each other a handshake. "Where's Tyrone?"

"Don't know. You trying to get something? 'Cause I got the good shit."

"Like what?"

"Somethin' to get high."

Jonathan felt annoyed. "No! Where's Trey?"

"He's there." Ray pointed to Trey's car.

"Okay. Later."

Jonathan rode his bike over to a blue BMW-635i. One of Trey's soldiers moved into Jonathan's path and stopped him.

"What do you want?"

"I need to speak to Trey."

"'Bout what?"

"Some business."

The guy turned to Trey and told him someone wanted to talk to him.

"Who's that?"

"Me, Jonathan."

"Oh, shit, what's up? Let him through. You are the *man* on the football field. You won me a lot of money."

"Really? Where's my cut?"

They laughed, and then Jonathan said, "I need to talk to you about my sister."

Trey got very serious. "Get in."

"What about my bike?"

"Nobody is going to take your shit!" yelled the driver.

"I don't want to leave it like that. This is my transportation. I don't want one of those crackheads to take my bike."

Trey told his driver to put the bike in the trunk of the car.

"What do I look like, a parking attendant? Fuck that bastard and his bike."

Trey gave the driver a look that said, "Don't fuck with me." The driver got out and put the bike in the trunk.

"That's right, put my shit in the trunk, with your bitch ass," Jonathan said.

Trey laughed and said, "This boy got heart."

Jonathan got into the back seat. He looked around, more than ready to shoot the driver and Trey, but he realized it wasn't the right time. Trey's crew had seen him get into the car. He didn't want anyone putting a price on his head because of a careless move. He explained to Trey that he didn't want his sister in the street and asked him not to give her any more credit to get drugs. He didn't want her to get beat up over something that could be prevented. Jonathan also asked if he could pay her debt and buy some drugs. Trey asked to see the money, and Jonathan showed him $5,000. Trey agreed.

Trey kept asking about Nina, saying she was the best fuck he'd ever had. Jonathan was mad, but he kept it under control. Trey went on in detail about how he'd wrecked that pussy. He told Jonathan that he owned her and she would never get out from under him.

Trey's driver took them to the safe house at Baisley Road, not far from Jamaica Avenue in Queens. They invited Jonathan inside. Jonathan paid Trey $500 for Nina's debt and also gave him $10,000 for some weed, pills, and cocaine. After they made the transaction, Trey walked Jonathan around the house.

This place is run like a factory, Jonathan thought. He realized that the drug trade could make him a lot of money.

Trey tried to get Jonathan to rejoin the Lil' Trouble Makers.

"No, thanks."

"You better not go out on your own with the drugs you just bought. And tell Nina, 'The dick is here anytime.' When she gets herself together, she'll be working for me."

Jonathan didn't dare say anything to Trey. He and the driver walked Jonathan to the BMW, and he got onto his bike and rode away.

Back at the house, Nina was awake, sitting and gazing into space.

"Are you feeling any better?

"No. I was worried about you."

"If you don't want *me* to worry, you shouldn't be on the street."

Jonathan gave her some of the drugs, but Nina wasn't herself. She had completely lost control. That's when he made up his mind to tell Tommy and Rico. He was going to get rid of Trey.

It was a long night for Jonathan. He had to control Nina and keep her from running out of the house. The more drugs he gave her, the worse she got. In the morning, he went to the basement to find Tommy and Rico. He told them what had happened, and that he'd tried to help, but it didn't work. He didn't understand the power of that drug.

Tommy and Rico got dressed and went to see Nina. Being detectives, they knew what to do. She fought both of them. They finally got her to calm down after a long battle. They were trying to keep it from the family. If the others heard, it wouldn't be good for any of them.

Jonathan, Tommy, and Rico took Nina to Field Rehabilitation Center, in West Hampton Beach. Nina kept calling Jonathan a traitor, which hurt him deeply.

Tommy walked into the medical center, gave them a stack of cash, and told them to take of Nina. He said he would be back in thirty days. On the ride home, Jonathan didn't say much. Tommy told him he'd done the right thing. It still made Jonathan feel like shit.

Yet with Nina out of the way, he could take care of Trey. He knew that going back to that house where Trey sold drugs was risky, so he came up with a plan to kill all of them. He would blow up the place.

He made ten pipe bombs the way Duke had taught him. Duke had given him about forty blocks of C-4. Jonathan used a high-grade aluminum pipe, inserted a nail in the middle, and packed the pipe with C-4. Because C-4 is extremely stable, he had to destabilize it, so he soaked it in vinegar. That would ensure that it blew up, even if there was a problem with the detonator cord. He had to be sure not to make any mistakes. He added the detonator cord to the blasting cap and a timer, just in case the detonator failed.

He believed the best method of delivery was to use his dogs, because nobody would suspect the dogs of doing anything wrong. Plus, Jonathan couldn't risk being seen by Trey's crew. He'd trained the dogs for two weeks until they were able to place the bombs where they needed to be. Each dog carried a bomb in its mouth, and every time a dog put a bomb in the right spot, it came back for the next one.

Jonathan stood on the side of the building across the street from Trey's drug house. Though his binoculars, he saw that everything was clear. He gave the order for Thunder and Lightning to put the bombs near the basement window, which had a half circle of metal around it to keep the water out. That would make a good buffer for the blast's blowback.

After Thunder and Lightning placed the bombs in the basement window, he met the dogs in the middle of the block. He gave the last four bombs to Thunder, one bomb at a time, then ordered him to the first level of the roof. It would have been better if Lightning had gone, but she was pregnant and about to have puppies.

Jonathan and Lightning slowly started walking away. Within two minutes, Thunder had returned from delivering the last bomb, and Jonathan set the timer by remote. He had a fifty-foot range. He believed that the bastard who had hurt Nina would pay a high price with his life.

Is this business or personal? Jonathan wondered. *It's a little of both.*

He stopped walking and looked around. He turned the switch on and pressed the firing button.

The next morning Jonathan read the newspaper report. One hundred and seventy-four people were killed after a house exploded in South Jamaica, Queens, on Thursday, officials said. Police and firefighters sifted through the rubble of the two-story home on Baisley Road in South Jamaica after the explosion razed the structure shortly before ten o'clock in the evening. One hundred and seventy-four people had been inside the house when it blew up. Eight other people outside the house were also injured. The victims were taken to three area hospitals. A woman, April, said the explosion shook her house. She further said that there was a lot of drug activity. The house had been illegally converted into a rooming house with at least eight rooms, which were being used to process drugs.

The cause of the explosion was under investigation. Brooklyn Union Gas spokesperson Wendy McKenzie said it appeared that a gas leak might have caused the explosion. Officials condemned the badly damaged houses on both sides of the explosion. Red Cross was assisting nineteen people in finding temporary shelter until the residents were allowed back into homes that were intact but might have been compromised.

Jonathan felt that no one would ever know what happened. *A gas leak,* he thought. *Nice.* His ego wasn't so big that he wanted to take credit for it.

A few days later, he called the rehab facility to check on Nina. "Hey."

"Hey, John John."

He smiled a little. "How do you feel?"

"I'm fine."

"Are they treating you okay?"

"Sure. I just want you to know I'm sorry for the pain I caused. I know now that you were helping me."

"You know I love you. I forgive you, but I was scared. That's why I told Tommy and Rico."

"I'm good with it. Tommy came a few days ago. I was happy to see him. I know there are so many secrets in that family."

"No shit."

"Well, I have to go," Nina said.

"Listen, did you hear what happened to Trey?"

"I heard he's dead. I have to go."

"Later."

Thunder and Lightning became the parents of five puppies, two males and three females. Jonathan had more than enough money to take care of them. He named one male King Ren, because he was so large at birth, and the other male Mr. Moe. He named the females Shadow, Ginger, and Allie. He felt very proud of them.

The next time Jonathan visited Sharon, they went upstairs to her room to watch TV. Sharon took off her jeans and got into bed. She told him to do the same and get in bed with her. He hugged her, and she started kissing him. Jonathan wasn't sure about going all the way with her. He was afraid she might not enjoy it or might somehow link sex with her father. He decided to let her take the lead.

"I think we should stop," he said.

"So, what? There's nothing wrong with people enjoying each other." She hugged him really tight.

Jonathan put his arms around her. She closed her eyes, and he kissed her.

"What was that?"

"What?"

"Have you been kissing other girls? Because the last time we kissed, it wasn't that good."

He smiled. "Just practicing kissing my hand."

He simply did what Nina had taught him, and the rest he made up as he went along. He traced his fingers up and down her chest and kept going until he reached under her blouse. She wasn't wearing a bra. He stroked her breasts, and she closed her eyes. He watched her reaction to make sure he didn't cross the line or make her feel uncomfortable.

"Are you okay?" he asked.

"Stop being nervous."

"I don't want to hurt you," he said.

"Love cannot hurt us, because you love me. Right?"

"Right. But if you feel a hint of pain, let me know. Don't let anyone do anything to you that is not pleasant."

"Fuck me and stop talking."

His fingers glided over her soft, warm skin until he reached her moist private parts. He paused for a second, but she didn't stop him.

"Remember, it's up to you how far you want to go," he said. "You can stop any time."

That calmed him and gave him more courage. He hesitated for another moment, then slowly pulled off her underwear. He took a deep breath and was getting really turned on. He had no problem going inside her and stroking her in and out with his fingers.

To his surprise, she got extremely excited. She moved him away, got up, and took off her top, and he also stripped off the rest of his clothes. They stared into each other's eyes. He grabbed her and kissed her. They fell back onto the bed, and Jonathan went inside her. It was tight and wet but okay. It was nothing like Lisa.

Jonathan moved slowly in and out of her, not wanting to hurt her, but she whispered, "I'm a woman. Stop fucking me like a kid."

Jonathan pulled out and flipped her over. He climbed on her back like a dog.

"That's better," she cried. "That's better."

After they finished, they held each other. Then he took a shower.

"Are you okay?" Sharon asked.

"I'm fine. You know I love you, right?"

"I know."

Sharon got back into bed and went right to sleep. He kissed her and let himself out. He got Tiger and walked back to the house. He wasn't sure how he felt about having sex with Sharon. He'd had no idea she was so aggressive. It bothered him a little. He got the feeling the relationship would not last.

When he turned the corner, he saw Tyrone. Tyrone had been in jail for two years on a drug charge. He had missed his brother Trey's funeral. As Tyrone got older, he'd started to look just like his brother.

"What's up?"

"All's good."

"Nice dog," Tyrone said. "Got me a pit bull. My brother told me he sold you some shit."

"He did?"

"Do you got it?

"Why?"

"I want to buy it from you on credit."

"I don't do credit. The answer is no, no credit. That's how my sister got in trouble."

"I heard."

"So you knew that he raped her."

Tiger had detected the tone of Jonathan's voice and started to bark at Tyrone.

"Yo, tell your dog to calm the fuck down, before I put a bullet in his ass. I knew. There was nothing I could have done. I was locked up."

"Forget it," Jonathan said. "Come with me. You can have it, I don't want no part of that shit. But I'm keeping the weed."

"What the fuck? You're going to give me almost a kilo for free? Truly, you're good brother. Shit, man, we can work together."

Jonathan knew why Tyrone was so excited. In three months, he would be sitting on $5 million. Fast money, fast cars, and even faster women.

"I don't want anything to do with it. Take it and don't come around me with no more bullshit."

"I hear you," Tyrone said. "If it means anything, I'm sorry."

"Me, too. I need to know that you understand me. I'm not with the drug shit. Because if you tell me anything other than you understand, we have a problem."

"Oh, shit, he got balls."

Jonathan paused and his eyes narrowed.

"Understand," Tyrone said.

Jonathan had Tyrone in his room and could have killed him. But his beef had been with Trey, and it had been dealt with. He gave Tyrone all of the cocaine.

"I'm gonna be rich," Tyrone said. "I'm gonna make a million dollars a week."

"I don't give a shit," Jonathan told him.

Tyrone walked way.

EIGHT

Jonathan grew up into a wonderful young man. He was now six feet tall and weighed about 190 pounds, with short curly hair and no facial hair yet. He felt happy that his body had started growing. He was taller than his father and all of his sisters. It was as if Michael Scicertti, the Swiss sculptor, had carved his body into a perfect form, with every muscle chiseled to perfection, showing its definition. He was sixteen years old and ready to conquer the world.

The sun's rays sparkled in blue and yellow on the window ledge. For the first time in a long while, Jonathan woke up with no real pressure or fears. He had worried about being caught and had started to feel conflicted about the things he had done. Moreover, it often bothered him at night, causing him to get only two to three hours of sleep a night. He had ordered his dogs to kill that white police officer, he'd shot Sharon's father three times and killed him, and he'd blown up Trey's drug house, killing 174 people.

But today he felt good. It was going to be a good day. He thought that if the police hadn't found out by now, it was just another cold case. At this point, he believed that the only way he'd get caught would be by confessing to what happened or if he told someone else and that person ratted him out to the police. He didn't hate cops, but he knew they couldn't catch a cold if they were running around butt naked in a snowstorm.

One day while walking to Sharon's house, he ran into Cindy. She was a nice girl, but she talked too much. Plus, she kept dwelling on suicide. She'd tried it once that Jonathan knew about. One day when

he'd been walking his dogs, he saw her in the park, crying, with her
wrists cut. There was blood on the ground and on her jeans. She made
him promise not to take her to the hospital, so he took her home and
tended to her knife wounds. He stayed with her all night, until she felt
better. He never thought he would run into her again.

"Hey, Johnnie."

"What's up?"

They greeted each other with a hug.

"Shit, you've gotten so big. You were just a baby last year. What
happened? I need a ride. You got a car?"

"No, I don't have a car."

"So, where you going?"

"To see my girl."

"The one I saw you with last week? I thought you guys were just
friends."

He hadn't realized someone was watching him. It was at that point
that he made up his mind to always *assume* someone was watching him.
Call it distrust or paranoia, but he would beware.

"What gave you that idea?" he asked.

"I saw you with her, and then I saw her hugged up with Tyrone at
the movies."

"What? No shit!"

"That's why you should be my man," Cindy said. "I will treat you
right."

Jonathan tried to control his fury, but he thought, *That bitch.*

"Can you please get your car and give me a ride? I'll give you gas
money."

"Okay, you have to listen to me," he said. "Go home, and get some
rest. I don't have a car."

"Are you mad at me?"

"No, I'm not mad at you. I need to take care of something. I'll
call you."

"Promise."

"No promises, but call me if you don't hear from me."

"Love you."

"Sure you do." Jonathan kissed her good-bye.

He made his way to Sharon's house, but when he got there, his key wouldn't fit the lock. He rang the doorbell and heard voices inside. He rang again, and Sharon opened the door.

"Hey."

"Hi."

"Come in," she said. "We need to talk."

Jonathan looked around and saw Tiger. The dog trotted over and sat next to him. Tyrone came downstairs, and Tiger started to bark.

"Shut the fuck up," Tyrone said. "I'm about sick of that dumb dog."

"I told you to stop talking to my dog like that," Sharon said.

"Like what? I'll talk to anybody any way I want."

Jonathan thought, *This has nothing to do with me. Anyway, this is not about anything. I love her, and it is what it is.*

"She loves me, not you," Tyrone boasted. "You're just some plaything to her."

Jonathan stared at Tyrone and thought that now his beef was with Tyrone, too. His heart sank into his chest, and he wanted to scream. After all he and Sharon had been through, and just like that, it was over. Jonathan knew that it wasn't him. She was sex crazy. That was cool, but he wished she had talked to him about it first.

"Hey, no problem. Sharon, you take care. I've gotta go."

"No. I want to talk about this." She reached out and tried to snatch his arm, and he pulled away.

"Give me a hug. Don't leave here mad," she said, choking on her words.

"Are you for real? There is nothing to talk about. You got your bad boy."

Tyrone turned to Sharon. "What the fuck is that supposed to mean? Yeah, I'm a bad boy 'cause I got money. And don't ever curse my girl."

"This is private, so fuck off," Jonathan said.

"I'll tell you later, baby." She reached out for Tyrone, and they held hands. "Just leave, Jonathan. You will always be special to me."

"Whatever! You're a mess, a confused bitch, and you will get what you deserve." Jonathan paused for second and yelled, "Special—fuck off! Whatever." He shook his head.

"You know, Jonathan, you're a real piece of shit," Sharon said. "It's no wonder you got your ass kicked every day by your sisters."

"What? You got your ass kicked by girls?" Tyrone said. "Oh, shit!"

"Have a nice life," Jonathan said. "I hope you're happy with everything you get. And before you start talking about my sisters, take a look at your own life."

"Just leave!" Sharon shouted. "You're a fucked-up person for trying to bring up old stuff. All I wanted to do was talk about this."

"I can't even guess what you would like to talk about."

Jonathan wanted to tell her how he felt about her. *Fuck her,* he said to himself. He was thinking too much and had to slow his mind down. His head started to hurt. He stood there without moving.

"You heard the lady," Tyrone said.

"Loud and fucking clear."

Jonathan stroked Tiger's head and said good-bye to the dog. He felt betrayed. It had been a few years, but they had been good years, because he knew that Sharon's father would never come back to hurt her and Ms. Renee. Jonathan felt okay that they would be safe, but he wasn't crazy about Tyrone and considered him a dangerous person.

As Jonathan walked back to his house, Tiger followed him. It wasn't a bad thing that they'd broken up, because Sharon was a little nutty anyway, and when Tyrone found that out, this would be Jonathan's revenge. He thought about it and then laughed to himself. He felt sad, but life goes on.

When he got back to the house, Nina was sitting on the bed, reading a novel. Her hair was pinned back, and she wore short pants and a blue T-shirt with no bra. He told her what had happened.

"Well, she's a fucking crazy-ass nut anyway. She needs to be locked up. Because that tampon shit was sad but funny, and if that was my daughter, I would have taken her to the insane asylum a long time ago, the dumb crazy bitch!"

"That's a little harsh, don't you think?"

"No. Fuck her! If she hurts you, she hurts me. Where is Renee with all of this? I'm sure she doesn't approve of Tyrone. Do you love her?"

"Yes and no. I do really, really like her."

"Are you going to fight for her?"

"No, I'm not a bad boy."

"What?"

"The last time we had sex, she wasn't happy."

Nina laughed and said, "You're only sixteen, and she's what? Eighteen? What the fuck do both of you know about sex? She probably can't fuck anyway. Did she at least give you a blow job?"

"No. She told me she's not a little girl and to fuck her like a woman."

"Okay, she's full of shit. The crazy bitch doesn't know shit. She needs help, her father fucked up her mind. Look, so what? You're a nice guy. What happened after you finished? Did she tell you she didn't like it?"

"No, she went to sleep."

"Listen, some of the best liars are women, but the one thing they'll never lie about is sex. They will let you know if you're wasting their time. Well, in my book, if you could put a woman to sleep after fucking her, you did a good job. There's nothing wrong with being a nice guy. Who wants their ass kicked all the time? See, every girl wants a bad boy until he starts beating her ass. You understand?"

"Yes, I understand."

"Does she like anything about you?"

"Well, at least she likes the way I kissed her."

"You learned from the best. Now I'll give you some tips, and you will be fine. Don't ever let a woman fuck with your head again. You're the man. Got it?"

"Got it."

Nina stood up and locked the door. She took off her jeans and gave Jonathan a "show and tell." She showed him how to touch and hold a woman. She told him a woman needed to feel that a man was in control and that he could handle her. Every now and again, he should spank her ass, but, "Don't start whaling away as if you're spanking a kid. Be easy, just enough to make that ass shake."

She went into the bathroom, and when she finished, Jonathan lay on the bed with his eyes closed. She climbed on top of him. He opened his eyes, as she started ride him.

"Just be in control, don't rush."

He nodded and stroked her back. "Do you think we should be doing this?"

"What do you think? Don't give a half-assed answer. Be a man. If you want it, ask me for it."

Not knowing what to say, Jonathan asked, "Can I have some pussy, please?"

They both started to laugh.

"You're so funny. I'm yours and will always be."

Within seconds, they were both naked. After they finished, Jonathan just lay on the bed with Nina in his arms. He thought about how much he liked her. He wasn't dwelling on Sharon.

Could I marry Nina? He laughed to himself. She looked good. She had put back on all of the weight she'd lost from her drug days. They both fell asleep.

The telephone rang. Jonathan woke up and reached for it.

"Hi, Johnnie."

"You sound funny. What's wrong?" Jonathan asked. He knew it was Cindy, because she was the only one who called him Johnnie.

"I . . . I killed myself."

"What the fuck are you talking about?" he said, confused.

"Come over."

"No. Cindy, what's wrong with you?"

"Fuck you. You can't tell me no."

"Why are you yelling at me? What's wrong?"

"Please, I don't want to die."

"Shit, what did you do?" Jonathan yelled.

"I really don't want to die."

"Be there in a minute."

He told Nina what was going on, and he grabbed some money.

Nina said she would drive him. They both got dressed and ran to the car.

"Why is my life so fucking hard?" Jonathan yelled and shook his head.

"I told you that the women you meet will be fucking crazy-ass bitches. Now you understand."

"When did you tell me that?"

"When we went to Ohio, remember? You said '*The story of my life, I'm surrounded by crazy ladies.*' And I said, 'You don't know how true that statement is.'"

"Yeah, I remember now."

By the time they arrived at Cindy's house, it was too late. Jonathan saw her mother on the street, screaming and crying. The New York City EMTs and the police were already there. Jonathan saw them bring Cindy out in a black body bag.

Nina assured him that there was nothing he could have done.

NINE

It was April, and Jonathan could barely contain his excitement. Graduation was only thirty days away, and next week he would leave to visit the University of Alabama in Tuscaloosa.

One morning before he went to school, he saw his family gathered in the living room. Tommy and Rico were playing cards, and Frankie J kept bragging about how much money he'd made last night. Anna looked high from cocaine. The rest of his sisters sat around talking to one another and counting cash, while Judy cooked some food in the kitchen.

Jonathan walked past Judy without speaking and approached his father. "Good morning, everybody."

"Hey, here's my boy. Are you using steroids? You got big. But I can still kick your ass."

Jonathan nodded and said, "Fine."

"Are you being smart?"

"No."

"I think you're trying to mock me. Are you trying to mock me, boy?"

"No." Jonathan thought, *This may not end well. My dad is trying to start a fight with me, but for what reason, I don't know.*

"Really."

"I'm going to Alabama to try out for the football team."

"Steroid boy, who told you that you could go to college?"

"Nobody, I'm just going."

"You can go to play whatever you like, but you're not going to college. You're going to work in the family business."

The family business consisted of five brothels in Freeport, New York, and a very profitable drug trade. Jonathan had heard that the business made from three to four million a month.

"With all due respect," Jonathan said, "the answer is no."

His father scowled. "What did you say to me?"

Jonathan's heart was set on going to college to get away from the family. "I think you heard me. I don't want to work for you," he said firmly.

Frankie J looked at Tommy. "Do you hear this shit?" He turned back to Jonathan and said, "I own you. You're an ungrateful piece of shit!"

Jonathan hung his head and said, "Can I go and try out, please?"

"You can do whatever the fuck you want, but after high school you're going to work for me. You got something to say?"

Jonathan kept his voice low because he didn't want to get the "animals" up and armed. "Okay."

"You know, I don't like your attitude. You should show me some respect."

"I respect you."

"See, you're being a real asshole. Get on your knees."

Jonathan didn't move. Frankie J stood up, and before Jonathan could say anything, his father punched him in the chin.

Jonathan crashed to the floor. He could hear Tommy in the background telling him not to move and to stay down. Jonathan stood back up, not realizing that this would show he was disrespecting the boss. Yet he didn't respect Frankie J for being the boss; he respected Frankie J for being his father.

Jonathan looked into his father's eyes. They no longer displayed signs of fatherly adoration or any affection he might have had for his son. Jonathan didn't see a compassionate human being. The sinister creature he stood face-to-face with disturbed him. Jonathan's father, Frankie J, had no humanitarian quantities that Jonathan could identify with. The evil that lived within Frankie J was deep-rooted, and Jonathan felt truly scared. While he stared at his father, he was literally looking at a reflection of himself, a person cut from the same monstrous cloth.

"You think you're better than us." Frankie J pointed around the room.

"No, I don't," Jonathan cried.

"Yes, you do, you think you're better than us. You're nothing to me, you're nothing but a punk. And I got something for punks like you."

Frankie J hit Jonathan again, and he fell to the floor. Judy jumped in and punched Jonathan. Frankie J and all of the other sisters, except Nina, began kicking him. Jonathan covered his face to protect himself. This beating was different. Up until now, his father had never hit him for what seemed like hours, and Jonathan had never begged them to stop. Regardless of how much it hurt, he refused to beg for mercy, because *the merciless will never show a person mercy unless it's for selfish reason*, he thought.

His father ordered the sisters to stop. Jonathan lay there for a few seconds.

"Now get on your knees."

Jonathan got on his knees with the help of Judy and Gail. Frankie J stood in front of him.

"If I took out my dick and shoved it in your mouth, you would be eternally grateful and would thank me for sparing your life. You think I forgot that you said to all of us, 'You all can line up and suck my dick'?"

"Hold his head," he ordered Gail.

Jonathan could hear Nina crying in the background and his sisters laughing at him, calling him all kinds of cruel names.

"Now, baster! Who's the boss?"

"You are!"

Frankie picked up his gun and put it to his son's head. Jonathan closed his eyes.

"After high school, what are you going to do?"

Jonathan paused, opened his eyes, and said, "Suck your dick?"

Tommy and Rico let out a hearty laugh, and Judy started laughing, which surprised Jonathan.

Frankie J hit Jonathan again and told everyone to be quiet. Everyone calmed down.

"I'm going to asked you one more time."

"I will be working for you."

Frankie hit Jonathan on the head with his gun again and sat down.

"I don't care how big you get, you're nothing to me. You hear me, motherfucker? You will appreciate what I'm going to do for you."

Jonathan walked backward, never taking his eyes off Frankie. "Whatever," he replied.

"I don't care about you. You're just another person to me. You had better get on the same page with us, or I will put you in your grave myself! Either way, I don't give a fuck. Get this piece of shit away from me. He thinks he's better than me. Well, I taught him. I'm the king, I'm better than he is."

While Jonathan walked away, he stumbled, and Judy yelled, "Tell that bitch Nina she's coming back to work, too."

Tommy and Rico helped Jonathan get up, and he saw Nina standing there with tears in her eyes. She didn't dare say a word for fear she might get beaten, too. She followed them to his section of the house.

As they walked away, Jonathan heard his father say, "Now that's how you break a person spirit. He's mine now!"

"That's right, baby," Anna said. "You're the man. The boy is nothing."

Tommy helped Jonathan onto his bed and told Rico and Nina to go into the other room.

"Hey, kid, listen, you know it's not me. Right?"

"Sure, Tommy. But I don't understand, why me?"

"We play the cards that we were dealt in this life."

"But we can fold and get out of the game, yes?"

"Yes, you can, but it will cost you more than you're willing to pay. It may cost your life. Here, this is for you."

Tommy handed him a set of car keys and told him the location of the car. It was a 1976 Oldsmobile Ninety-Eight Regency coup. "It's yours. Think of it this way: you will be the only high school boy with a great job."

"You're funny, Tommy. Great job, I don't think so. Thanks for the car."

"Not just a car, it's a driving machine."

"Did you at least take out the eight-track?"

"Yes, I did. You'll be okay, but watch your back. It's not over with you and him."

"Tommy, thank you so much."

"You're very welcome, kid."

Jonathan wasn't happy with how things were going. He asked Nina to explain what had happened out there with Frankie J. Nina told him that it was Frankie J's way of controlling his people. Sometimes he even put the date rape drug, flunitrazépam, in someone's drink and would videotape and take pictures of the person performing all kinds of humiliating acts.

"He'll embarrass you until you submit, or he will kill you," Nina said. "It's his way of keeping you in the gang and controlling you. He likes to manipulate people so that they'll be loyal. It happens to everyone who joins his gang. If you're not loyal to him, you will die."

Nina told him that people were not loyal in the true sense of the word *loyalty*, but they could never be free of Frankie J, because of those pictures and videos of sexual acts he'd recorded. She said she was sure that the camera had been rolling this morning, while Frankie J beat up Jonathan.

"He cut you a break today," Nina said, "but it will happen, and that's why you have to be careful. Initiation night is going to get crazy once they accept you into the gang. The only way out is death."

Jonathan went down to the basement and behind the wall where he had built a safe. He pulled out his Titanium Gold .50 AE caliber Desert Eagle. He loaded the clip with eight bullets, put the clip in the gun, and went into the bathroom. He decided that he would rather be dead than work for Frankie J. He would never submit to his father, nor would he allow Frankie J to kill him.

Jonathan sat on the toilet and contemplated ending his life. When he made the decision to kill himself, he didn't want anyone to know.

Nina was in the other room with Thunder and Lightning. Thunder pushed the door open with his nose and looked at Jonathan.

Jonathan said, "Goodbye, my friend."

Thunder began barking frantically. Jonathan paused, still sitting on the toilet. Nina came through the bathroom door. Lightning followed her and started howling like a wolf.

When Nina saw him with the gun, she asked, "Jonathan, what are you doing?"

"Nothing."

"Why do you have a gun?"

"I'm not going to live Frankie's life. I'm just not going to do it. It's the only way out."

"That's not the way, Jonathan. What the fuck is wrong with you? This is not how you go about things in the face of what frightens you. You have to be a man. You think I'm not scared for you?"

"I can't do it. I'm going to die."

"Then you will go to hell. You will go straight to hell. Is that what you want?"

"At least in hell I won't deal with Frankie's bullshit." Jonathan put the gun to his head.

Nina yelled, "Suicide will free your body from the realities of life, but it will imprison your soul to eternal damnation in a pit of fire and unrest! You told me that one day. Don't do it. Give me the gun. It's not the way. You're a warrior, a leader." Nina paused. "Think back to when you were in Montana doing the vision quests. Let nature speak to your heart. You have a power not many men possess. Please don't leave me!"

Jonathan thought about how wrong it would be to leave her. Not that she was helpless, but he cared for her.

Nina fell on her knees. "I love you, and that should be enough for you to stay with me."

Jonathan stood up, and Thunder watched every move he made. He paused, then handed Nina the gun. She and the two dogs ran out of the bathroom. When she came back, she held him tight.

"Don't ever do that to me again."

"Sorry."

"I forgive you. Jonathan, I want you to know that I love you, and if you decide to run, I'll run with you, and we'll be together always. If you want to stay and fight, whether we win or lose, I'll be with you."

"Do you know that ever since I was in the woods doing the vision quest, whenever something dangerous is about to happen, I can feel it in my soul. I'm not scared because I know I'll be safe from any harm or physical danger. And I'll keep you safe. I won't let you down. I'll never leave you, and that's my word."

Nina put her hand on his chest and said, "We're going to be okay. It won't always be like this."

When she touched his chest, it reminded Jonathan of another time when he had been severely beaten. *I came home from school early one day and saw my sisters in the backyard, soaking up the sun. When they saw me, they chased me for no reason. Judy grabbed me, and they took me into the garage. They duct-taped my mouth and tied my hands behind my back. Gail took off my shoes and socks. My other sisters held me as I fought for my life. I tried to move, but I couldn't. They were much stronger than I.*

Judy took an electric cable and whipped the bottoms of my feet. It was a searing and burning intense pain. The sensation of pain radiated through my whole body, and I passed out. When I came to, I could barely walk out of the garage. The sun blinded me, but I still could see my sisters drinking beer and joking about what they had done to me.

I walked over to Sharon's house, but she wasn't there. Ms. Renée answered the door. She could see that something was wrong with me, and I remember falling into her arms. I slept for hours, and when I woke up she was still holding me. She put her hand on my chest and said, "We're going to be okay."

Nina ran the water for a bath. While Jonathan soaked in the hot water, he started to wonder about his father. *That's weird. Why's he so crazy? I could call the police on them, but who would listen? Tommy and Rico are police officers. Plus, if Frankie goes to jail, he will hunt me down. There's no other way. If I run, I'm sure Frankie J will find me and then kill me. Just shooting up the place won't work, there's not enough firepower, but nevertheless, they all need to die. This is just too fucking much for a young man. I should be out getting some pussy or smoking weed.*

Nina came into the bathroom with two glasses of wine. "Don't go to school today. You don't look well. Drink this."

"I'm in so much pain. It just hurts."

"I know," Nina said.

"I don't understand. Why me? You know, all this time I believed that Frankie loved me, because I'm his son. All this time I knew that in some twisted way, he had my back and he wouldn't hurt me."

"Frankie J doesn't give a shit about anybody. If it's not about money, then he couldn't care less. Hey, listen, it's going to be okay. We have each other. Say the word, and we'll make a move on all of them," Nina said jokingly.

"Non è una buona idea" ("Not a good idea"). Jonathan and Nina had learned several languages over the years. His Italian was a little weak, but he whispered to Nina, *"Ucciderli tutti"* ("Kill them all").

"I know." She paused, looking him in the eyes. "One day."

"Yes, one day."

"Will you tell me where you got that gun from?"

"Sure, I will, but not now. Do you know what kind of work I'll be doing for Frankie?"

"Mostly, you'll be at the bar and watching the money. It's a whorehouse. You can get all the pussy you want."

"I don't want to do it, and most of all I don't want to have sex with no old women."

"I don't blame you. What are we going to do?"

That question got his attention. *Is she spying on me?* he wondered. He really wanted to believe that her question was out of concern and nothing else. *I would feel fucked up if I had to kill her.* Jonathan had never had any reason not to trust Nina, but now he didn't know. *Could Frankie J be smart enough to put a spy on me? If he did, that's not good. She doesn't really know anything. I have more on her than she does on me. Shit! She was gone for thirty days, and nobody asked about her. I'll just keep my eyes open.*

Nina punched Jonathan on the arm and asked, "Where are you?"

"Sorry, just thinking. You know, I'm going to Alabama next week for a few days and then graduation, and I guess I'll be working."

"Do you have a way out?"

"How? I don't want to die over no bullshit. I know that I don't want to be a gangster. It's not me. That's not my life. Will it always be like this?"

"We don't always get what we want. Love you."

"Nina" . . . Jonathan paused.

"Yes."

"When you went away, how come nobody asked about you?"

"Tommy told them that he sent me on a vacation as a gift. Why?"

"Just asking." He played it off as normal curiosity. "I love you, too!" Nina got undressed and climbed into the bath.

"This feels good," she said. "Hold me. Don't ever do that to me again. Yes?"

"Yes. Nina, I will never let you go. I will always be here for you."

They had more wine, and Nina fell asleep in Jonathan's arms. He dozed off as well.

He dreamed of a pungent smell, old decaying flesh that irritated his nose. It was so horrifically revolting, his nose bled. With each breath, he struggled to take in air. It was an unspeakable, appalling stench. He was standing in a room he had never seen before, near a sign that read, "To change your life, some people who hurt you must be moved out of the way. To achieve this, some just might have to die." When Jonathan turned to walk away, a person with no facial features, dark tanned skin, and a white and red robe took him by the arm, handed him a key, pointed to a door, and said, "Open it." Jonathan complied and walked into the room. It was dark, with only a negligible amount of light.

"What is this place?" Jonathan asked.

A deep male voice said, "It's called the room of revenge. Revenge will make you feel better."

"So, who are you?"

"Just here to help you along."

"Help?"

"Yes. Help."

Jonathan looked around the room and saw Frank, his father; Anna Maria, his stepmother; and his stepsisters Gail, Anna, Maria, Paula,

Taren, and Alicia. He wondered why Judy wasn't there with them. They each had thick chains wrapped around their ankles. They hung upside down, six feet off the ground. They were all naked, with their hands stitched to the sides of their bodies.

People were positioned behind them, wearing hoods that covered their faces and brownish-red robes that looked like dried blood. These hooded individuals were beating Jonathan's family with whips made of wooden spikes and rusty nails. Blood dripped from their bodies. They cried out in pain. Jonathan could only think that this was their punishment for being such wicked, malicious people. He noticed that his stepmother, Anna Maria, wore a slight smirk. He thought, "That's about the right expression," because of her sadomasochistic lifestyle.

The deep voice told Jonathan that for him to live, they must die. He looked around again, and they made an impassioned plea for their lives. There was another sign with the following message: "Press the button, and they all die." Jonathan didn't see a button, but he saw Judy standing with her head hanging down.

He walked over to her and said, "You should be ashamed of the way you treated me."

She kept her head down and said, "Help me."

"At the right time, they will all die," Jonathan told himself, "but only on the terms that I dictate for them."

He woke up with sweat all over him. Nina had gone to get a towel to wipe him off and now stared at him. They didn't speak for a while.

Finally, she said, "I will support you. But you must constantly be cautious with your actions because you will never know who's observing you or who is eavesdropping on your conversations, so watch your back at all times."

A white light took Jonathan to the ceiling. He closed his eyes and heard, "You're not ready yet." Then the light let him go.

He woke up—this time for real—and Nina was still asleep. He woke her and they got dressed, had some more wine, and ate. He tried to get himself together. He knew it had only been a dream. The telephone rang.

"Hello," Nina answered.

"Hey, girl, it's me. Where's my boy?" Ms. Renee asked.

"He's here."

Nina gave the phone to Jonathan, whispering, "It's Renee." He waved his hands and arms like a crazy man. He didn't want to talk to Ms. Renee, because he didn't want to hear anything about Sharon.

"He's not talking."

"Put his ass on the phone," Renee demanded.

Nina covered the receiver. "She wants to talk to you."

Jonathan took the phone. "Hey."

"Are you okay? Sharon told me what happened."

"There was nothing I could do or say. I still care for her, and I don't want her to leave me."

"For the record, I would have gone for the nice guy. I don't want any more bad boys in my life. It was a living hell with James. I'm so glad he never came back. Thank you for that."

"Are you really happy without him?"

"Yes, I am. Now my daughter is making the same mistakes I made, and I truly hope she sees the light soon and finishes college."

"It might work out for her, I don't know," Jonathan said.

"Sure. See you at the graduation. I've got something for you. Also, thanks for keeping Tiger for me."

"Any time."

TEN

As a stream of acceptance letters arrived in the mail, Jonathan couldn't stop grinning. He realized, *I can choose any college I want.*

He tried to wear a poker face around his father and sisters, though. They always looked annoyed to see him in a good mood.

He ran into his bedroom. Nina lay across the bed, drinking wine and listening to music. Jonathan jumped and did a back flip onto the bed, spilling her wine.

"Boy, what the hell is wrong with you?"

"Everything. Look at these letters." He tossed them in the air, and they fell all over the bed.

Nina stood up and took off her wine-stained top. "Look what you did. What's going on with you?"

"I got accepted by some of the best football colleges."

"Hey, calm down, boy."

"I was offered academic and athletic scholarships to Florida State University, University of Oklahoma, Louisiana State University, Texas A&M University, and Ohio State University. Tuskegee Institute will grant me a full scholarship to play football only. New York University will award me an academic scholarship to get a master of science in international business, in conjunction with my bachelor of science degree at whatever undergraduate university I choose to attend."

"You are the man, baby. But you're crazy—you spilled my wine."

With the advanced placement classes I took in high school, he thought, *I'll have a bachelor's of science and a master's of science degree in less than three years. Love it!*

He took the bottle of wine off the nightstand and drank until the bottle was empty. "Open another one, and turn up the music."

He jumped up and down on the bed like a little boy. Nina joined him, and they bounced to the beat of the music and drank wine until they both passed out.

Jonathan didn't particularly care which college he went to, as long as it was in the South and far away from Queens, New York. He wanted to play for the University of Alabama, which had an excellent football program. The school didn't offer him a scholarship, but it did invite him to try out for the football team. If he made it, he would receive a full athletic scholarship. One of the biggest problems with the University of Alabama was that he might not get to play football until his third year, and he hoped to be finished with his studies by then. Yet planning to go to college comforted him, because he might have a chance to escape from his dysfunctional family.

Jonathan decided to leave for Alabama seven days earlier than the scheduled date. That way, he could see the campus and relax his mind. He called SWS On-Demand Charter Private Jet Service. Since this might be his only visit to a college, he wanted to enjoy the ride.

He pulled Tommy aside and asked, "Would you use your credit card to make me a reservation for a flight from Teterboro to Tuscaloosa, Alabama?"

"No problem, I'd be happy to," Tommy said. "I'm just sad Frankie J. won't let you go to college. You're a smart kid. You've come a long way. I'm proud of you."

Jonathan had told Tommy he really wanted to study international business and foreign policy—along with playing football. Jonathan had always loved Tommy.

I wish we were family, Jonathan thought. *Along with Nina and Rico. But no matter what happens, I'm not going to be like my father. I won't be part of a crime family, not for any amount of money.*

It was a daily struggle to fight the temptation of evil, being with his family.

On the morning of his flight, Jonathan woke up to the alarm. As he reached out, his hand bounced around like a poorly dribbled basketball until he found the off button. He rolled over and kissed Nina on the cheek.

"Wake up," he said. "It's three o'clock."

He sat on the edge of the bed and turned his attention to his dreams. He often woke up in a state of confusion because of them. Although his dreams were all different, they all ended the same way: with him being pulled to the ceiling by a white light and a voice saying, "You're not ready yet." Then he would be dropped to the ground, which always woke him up.

He and Nina took a shower and ate. The limousine Tommy had reserved pulled up to the house. Jonathan had decided to leave early in the morning to avoid seeing Frankie and the family.

A few days ago, Jonathan had put his guns, some of his money, and his important papers in a safe deposit box at Chase Bank. His checking account had a balance of around $20,000. He opened two additional accounts with United Bank Switzerland and Swiss National Bank. He liked the Swiss banks because, despite his age, they didn't ask many questions.

He also liked the Swiss because Switzerland had a politically and socially stable economy, with a reliable legal system and a history of economic prosperity. He trusted that his money would be safe there. His Uncle Duke had taught him how to open accounts with offshore banks. He deposited $50,000 in each bank account and kept $20,000 in cash with him. All of this money was his reward for keeping Tommy and Rico's secret.

Jonathan brought along the documents his grandmother Aiyana had given him. He wanted to review them when he had some time to himself. He thought, *Maybe I can make a few dollars.*

In the limousine, Nina kept staring at him.

"What's the matter?" Jonathan asked.

"Why?"

"You're looking at me like you have something to say. So, tell me what's on your mind."

"I'm sorry we can't have a normal life."

"What do you mean?"

"I mean, if you went to college and got a good job, we could have a normal life. You know."

"I know."

"But we have to work for Frankie." Tears flowed down Nina's cheeks. "Jonathan, all I know is your love, and I know you love me."

"I don't understand. What do you want me to do?" He felt annoyed.

"I want you to do something!"

"Like what?"

"Like fucking do something."

"Like what, Nina? You know I'm doing the best I can. I'm sixteen fucking years old, and every fucking day that I've been alive has been a fight. Did it ever occur to you that I want something better for our future?"

"So, protect our future."

"How do you suppose I do that?"

"I don't know."

"What's up with you, anyway? You know exactly what the fuck I'm up against. Are you pregnant?"

"No. Sorry." She put her arms around his waist, buried her head in his chest, and said, "I don't want to argue with you. I just want you to be a man and protect us from what's to come."

"We don't know what's to come, but I got you. You know, Nina, I want the crowd to scream, 'Go, Johnny, go!' Maybe just one time."

"I just want us to be a family one day. I want to have your children."

He smiled. This issue with his father was problematic, and to get out of working for a crime family, he might have to kill everyone. The planning of this had to be precise, or it could end Jonathan's life. After the thought of killing everyone crossed his mind, Jonathan realized it might be a mistake. He didn't want to do anything reckless. He had to rethink his actions. Killing his family would forever alter his life. But they just had to go. Death was the only solution.

"Nina, don't worry," Jonathan said. "It's going to be okay."

"I know," Nina responded. "Promise me."

"I promise. I'll take care of you."

When they arrived at Teterboro Airport in New Jersey, it reminded Jonathan of the first time he had flown in a private jet to Ohio.

Nina pulled him close to her and whispered, "Stay away from those nasty girls. There's really bad venereal disease in the South, so don't let your dick get in your line of reasoning. But have fun."

They both laughed.

"I'm going to miss you. I do love you, and you stay out of trouble, too."

As he walked toward the plane, he turned and blew a kiss to Nina. Then he climbed onto the jet.

The interior had four pairs of seats with a table in between each pair, and two black leather Chesterfield sofas on each side of the cabin. With its mahogany walls, the cabin of this private jet was reminiscent of yachts built in the 1930s.

Soft music played in the background. Jonathan saw an older woman reading the *Wall Street Journal*. A classic beauty, a white lady, with shoulder-length black hair. She had a small frame, her skin glowed, and her makeup was flawless. Although she didn't wear much jewelry, Jonathan could tell that the items she had on were extremely expensive. He imagined that if an artist could paint her portrait, it would win one of the country's highest honors, the National Medal of Arts. She was elegant.

"Hello."

"Hi."

"My name is Jonathan."

"I'm Nancy Meyer."

He sat in the seat in front of her. The flight attendant took Jonathan's overnight bag and put it in a closet. Then she asked them if they would like something before they taxied to the runway. Jonathan thought that six o'clock in the morning was a bit early to be drinking alcohol, but he said, "I'll take a gin and pink grapefruit juice."

Nancy said, "A scotch and soda, please."

Jonathan paused, then questioned, "May I ask what type of business you are in?"

"I'm a real estate developer and an attorney," Nancy said. "And you?"

"I'm a student."

"Student? On a private plane?"

"Yes. It's the only way to travel."

They both laughed.

"Where are you headed?"

"To Alabama for football tryouts."

"Crimson Tide."

"Yes. Crimson Tide. You know the team."

"I know it well. I went to Auburn. I'm a Tiger," she proudly stated.

"Well, you know if I get accepted to play football there, we will become natural enemies, right?"

"Even enemies can get along."

"I hear that. I hope to see you at the Iron Bowl."

"It's the best college football rivalry game played in the State of Alabama: The University of Alabama Crimson Tide and the Auburn University Tigers."

"What does a real estate attorney do?" Jonathan asked.

"I help people start new businesses. My firm does research for people, and if you get into legal trouble, I will get you out of it."

"Really? So what you're saying is, if I have a real estate issue, I could hire you for about an hour?"

"Sure."

"How does that work?"

"I get one thousand dollars an hour."

Cool as ice, Jonathan said, "Okay, I want to hire you."

"Really."

"Yes. I'm serious." Jonathan reached into his pocket and pulled out a wad of cash. He handed her $1,000.

Her eyes widened, then she smiled. She took out a pad and hand-wrote a receipt, signed and dated it, and gave it to him. "What do you want me to do?"

"I'd like you to read some documents and give me your opinion."

"Okay."

Jonathan told her about the properties his grandmother had left him in Montana, as well as the one in Italy. He pulled his overnight bag from the closet and opened it, then gave her a package that contained a last will and testament; the deed to land in Montana, which included all mineral rights; and legal papers stating that he was to be named president and owner of Russo's Olive Oil Company in Cetona, Italy.

Nancy reviewed each document. "What do you want to do with the land?"

"I'm not interested in becoming the president of an olive oil company in Italy," Jonathan said. "And I don't want to take care of land in Montana. I want to sell the land, but I don't know what to do with the olive oil company yet."

"I can help you sell it. We need a contract. I'll fax the document over to my team and let them start on the paperwork."

She instructed the pilot to land in Knoxville, Tennessee, where one of her satellite offices was located.

At the office, Nancy asked a staff member to take Jonathan to buy a suit.

"Make it a good one," she said. "I want you dressed to impress."

When Jonathan and the staff member returned, they made their way to the conference room. Jonathan saw papers spread all over the table.

"Nancy, what's up?"

"Did you know you have a gold mine here?"

His heart started to race. "I'm not sure what you're talking about. I don't understand."

He scanned a working draft of the contract. According to the law, he owned it all. He would become an instant millionaire.

"You own seventy thousand acres of land on the Blackfoot reservation," Nancy said. "That includes the mineral rights. The United State Geological Survey, in conjunction with the United State Army Corp of Engineers, has determined that there are 35 million barrels of oil under the surface of that land. At $25.26 a barrel, that comes to $884 million."

Jonathan interrupted her. "This is too good to be true! I don't know how to feel. It's a dream."

"I'm not finished," Nancy said. "The town constructed an

unauthorized casino on 240 acres of your land. Based on the financial statements, it's a very profitable casino, with a hotel and a motor lodge containing a total of 973 guest rooms, ten restaurants, and a gourmet coffee bar."

"Holy shit," Jonathan said. "Here, let me see that."

He scrutinized the financial statements and noticed that they reported $1 billion in unrestricted cash and $16 billion in gross sales.

"Where is the bathroom?"

"Down the hall, make a right," the clerk said.

In the lavish men's room, Jonathan stared into a mirror. Every fiber of his being pulsated with expectation. Adrenaline ran wild through his body. *If I become a millionaire, I'll be able to take care of Nina and get away from my family.*

After dinner, Nancy and Jonathan went back to work. By midnight, they had written the final draft of the contract.

At four o'clock in the morning, the contract was completed.

"The way I see it, you have two choices," Nancy said. "You can either claim ownership of the Great Wolf Casino and Resort, or you can take the money."

Hell, I'll take the money, Jonathan thought, but he didn't reveal this to Nancy. *Better play my cards close to the chest. I'm swimming with the sharks now. For the first time in a long while, I'm not worrying about the past or feeling anxious about the future. I'm truly happy right now.*

Without warning, he jumped up on the table, pumped his fist high in the air, and yelled, "I am the motherfucking man!"

The other lawyers cheered him on, chanting, "You are the man!" as Jonathan did a victory dance on the conference room table.

"Okay, let's get ready," Nancy said with a smile.

By 4:30 a.m., they were at the airport. It was a four-hour flight to Montana and a twenty-minute drive to reach the main offices of Gray Wolf Casino and Resort. Nancy, Jonathan, and a staff of twenty lawyers would be right on time for the 9:00 a.m. meeting.

At the casino, Jonathan recognized Chief Clayton.

"Jonathan! Wow, you've grown so much. Let me look at you."

They embraced.

"How are you, Chief Clayton?"

"Well, Jonathan, I'm very surprised about this whole thing. You could have called me, and I could have wired you a few dollars."

Jonathan forced a little laugh. "I just found out last night that it's my family's property."

"I know, son. Let's get this over with," Chief Clayton said in disgust.

Jonathan knew that the tribe was never going to play fair. He was glad he'd brought lawyers.

After the board of directors reviewed the contract prepared by Nancy, Chief Clayton looked at Jonathan and asked, "What do you want?"

Nancy said, "What's your offer?"

They discussed making Jonathan the chief financial officer after college and paying for his schooling. The board of directors would give Jonathan $3 million and would pay all of the legal fees.

Nancy whispered, "Do you want the money?"

Jonathan said, "Yes."

He looked around the boardroom, and for the first time in his life, he saw people for who they really were. These people did not have his best interests at heart, even the beloved Chief Clayton. They were literally trying to steal what was rightfully his. Because the tribe would pay Nancy, she could care less about Jonathan.

Just as she got ready to speak, Jonathan interrupted her. "I think I would like to take the money. However, three million dollars is insulting."

"What do you mean?" Chief Clayton asked.

"I want one billion dollars."

The men and the women in the room burst out laughing.

When the noise died down, Jonathan said it again: "I want one billion dollars."

The room got very quiet.

Chief Clayton asked, "Jonathan, can I talk to you alone?"

Jonathan leaned over toward Nancy. "What do you think?"

"No way should you be alone with him."

"With all due respect, Chief, whatever you have to say, do it in front of my lawyers."

"Okay, Jonathan, if that's what you want, then who the fuck do you think you are? Coming into my house, trying to take my fucking business. You've lost your mind. There's no way you will get one penny from me. You are nothing but a disrespectful little boy in a man's world."

The years of verbal and physical abuse by his family had hardened Jonathan to the point where Chief Clayton's words did not pierce the walls of his heart.

"Despite what you think, this is my property, this is my land. I will shut this place down and burn it to the fucking ground."

"Jonathan, we are family," Chief Clayton said.

"No! We are not."

Chief Clayton whispered to his lawyer, and the lawyer looked at Jonathan.

"You broke my heart."

"As you did mine, Chief."

Jonathan was about to respond again, but Nancy stopped him.

Chief Clayton's lawyer said, "Let's make this right."

Chief Clayton nodded in defeat, as Jonathan celebrated in his mind. *Triumph over evil,* he thought.

When the negotiations were over, Jonathan peered at a computer terminal as the chief wire-transferred $550 million into Jonathan's Swiss accounts. The tribe paid all of the legal fees.

No further words were exchanged between Jonathan and Chief Clayton. Jonathan walked out of the room a rich man.

"It was great meeting you and working with you," Nancy said.

"Likewise," Jonathan said, still in shock over what had happened in the meeting.

"Can I give you a ride?"

"I'm good." He kissed her on the cheek, and they went their separate ways.

He flew to Birmingham–Shuttles-Worth International Airport for a refueling and then to Tuscaloosa Regional Airport. On the flight to Tuscaloosa, he threw up a few times, as it finally hit him. *I am a rich man.*

His mind in turmoil, he was barely aware of either flight. His entire life had changed in the space of a few hours.

He hailed a taxi and told the driver, "University of Alabama campus."

Jonathan was the first student to arrive. He tried to switch gears in his mind, to put the previous day's events on a back burner. Now he had to concentrate on college. His sole purpose was to get a full scholarship. Despite the offers from other colleges, he wanted to be in the South.

It was 85 degrees, and approximately five hundred players were trying out for the University of Alabama Crimson Tide on the first day. Everyone was basically getting to know everyone else and becoming acquainted with the football coaches. The students each received a jersey and the necessary equipment, and the coaches gave them their room assignments.

The days were long and hot. The nights were just as hard, as the boys intensely studied complicated football plays and strategies. Jonathan believed that the football coaches pushed them to the max to weed out the weaker players.

Jonathan kept to himself. He didn't want to make any friends. The coaches ran those young men until players started to throw up and pass out or quit. The coaches kept saying that practice wouldn't be over until at least five people quit. One by one, students dropped out fast.

People have to be really special to rise to the next level as they go through life, Jonathan thought. *Just because they're great at a subject or a sport at age seventeen doesn't mean their success will last. When they recognize this, they can move on with life. The next level of greatness is not for everyone. Just because you were good in high school doesn't mean you can play college-level football.*

Jonathan impressed the coaches, and it earned him a spot on the team. He wanted all expenses paid, but they offered only to pay tuition, and he would not get to play on the team until he was a junior in college.

Yet he wanted to play now. He was in great shape. He was good enough to start *and* to get a free ride. He knew he could get an all-expense-paid trip at Tuskegee Institute in Alabama.

On the last day, the new freshmen were supposed to play the starting lineup. Jonathan felt great. Bryant–Denny Stadium was packed with forty thousand people in the stands. It was supposed to be a friendly scrimmage game, rather than the older players trying to kill the young ones.

Despite everything, Jonathan did a great job. He was the only player to score two touchdowns. The running back coaches wanted him to sign a letter of intent, but he said he would get back to them.

As a going-away gift, the Crimson Tide Spirit Squads threw a party for the football team to celebrate and blow off steam.

In the Spirit Squads clubhouse, Jonathan saw Lisa and walked over to her.

"Hey, you don't remember me, do you?" Lisa said.

"I do. What are you doing here?"

"I go to school here. Why else would I be here, silly?"

"I didn't know pole dancing was a major."

"Fuck you."

"You wish."

"Shit, you got big."

Jonathan turned to walk away.

"So it's like that, you're not talking to me."

Jonathan turned and looked at her. "Why should I talk to you? You fucked up my life."

"Just get over it. You know you're acting like a fucking bitch. I bet you could handle this pussy now."

"Not going to happen. I would rather fuck my dog in the ass without a rubber than you. Asshole!"

"You think you can fuck me, then leave me? No, sir, I own you."

"What? Stop the bullshit."

"Okay, let's just be friends."

They hugged. Lisa asked him for some money, and he gave her a few dollars.

"Thank you, baby. I'll see you on campus. But at some point you need to hit this ass again. You're the best lover I ever had."

"You're a real dumb ass. Look, I have to go. You're one sick person if you think I'm fucking you again. Get that through that big-ass head of yours."

Jonathan thought, *Best lover? Doesn't make any sense to me. It still hurts, what happened between us. Just because I've been away from someone who hurt me years ago doesn't mean the hurt is gone.*

"I see you looking at my friend. Hey, Zoe, come here."

Zoe walked over to Jonathan and smiled. He watched her shapely body moving with such grace. Her mysterious brown eyes glowed as she stared at Jonathan.

Like sexy innocence, he thought. She was small, with long black hair, a pretty face, and an athletic body. He guessed she was maybe twenty years old, about five feet four inches tall. She was by far one of the nicest-looking women he had seen in a while.

An older football player called Lisa over, and she left.

"Hey," Zoe said. "So, are you going to come here?"

"Only if I get a full scholarship."

"I take it you're from New York," she said.

"And you?"

"I'm from New Jersey. You're a long way from home."

"You, too."

"I had to get away from the family, you know."

"I know."

"How do you know Lisa?"

"We lived in the same neighborhood, in Queens, New York."

"She's cool—just a bit of a pain in the ass," Zoe said, rolling her eyes. "But she's okay. She really needs to get a job. She's always asking for money."

"I hear you." He nodded in agreement, thinking, *This is a big school. What were the odds of me meeting Lisa here?*

During the next two hours, Zoe poured out her life story to Jonathan, and he couldn't keep his eyes off her. She was a middle child. Her older brother, Robert, was sent to New Jersey state prison for rape and murder. Her young sister, Paola, had been admitted to John Hopkins Hospital Psychiatric Ward in Baltimore, Maryland. Her wealthy family owned about twenty-two gas stations on the East Coast. They were originally from San Vicente, Ecuador. She said she was majoring in international business, and this was her third year in college.

They decided to go back to her place to hang out. She lived in the Bluff Apartments on the University of Alabama campus.

At the apartment, she kicked off her shoes. "Want some wine?"

"Sure," Jonathan said, staring out the window. She had a great view of the campus.

Zoe sat on the bed, poured two glasses of wine, and handed one to Jonathan. He took off his shoes and wandered around the large one-bedroom apartment. He stopped to look at her family photos.

"This school makes me want to come here," Jonathan said. "I like it."

"Don't be sucked into its bullshit. If you don't have money, or you're not a superstar jock on full scholarship, then you won't be happy. That's what they do to the ball players here. Suck you in, and when you want out, they make it very hard to transfer. Be careful."

She refilled their wine glasses. "Come sit next to me. Are you afraid of me?"

"Why do you ask?"

"Because most guys would have tried to kiss on me by now, and I would be fighting them off me."

"Well, I'm not most guys."

"Fair enough."

The truth of the matter was, Jonathan felt a little intimidated by her because he didn't like aggressive woman.

They started doing shots of vodka. When they kissed, she was very responsive, but Jonathan took it slow and easy. He felt very relaxed, and she held him tight. After twenty minutes of foreplay, she pushed his head between her legs.

Eating pussy was very new to him. *Not really sure how to do it*, he thought, *but I'll give it a try*.

She moved her body up closer to the head of the bed, lying on her back with her knees at her shoulders and her legs spread wide open. He went downtown, and her body responded well. Jonathan's face was buried in her, and all he heard was "*No se detienen!*" ("Don't stop!")

She got very excited and moaned in ecstasy. She told him to be as nasty as he liked, and she got wet and sloppy fast. She let out a shriek.

He got on top of her, and after he was finished, he rolled over and kissed her.

They lay on the bed. He felt very relaxed, and all the stress of the world just melted away at that moment.

"I never had a lover like you. I feel so rejuvenated." She climbed on top of him. "You really don't know what you're doing, do you?"

"First time, you know!"

They both laughed.

"You're so easy to love," he said. "You have a calming spirit. It's easy to make love to you, even if I don't know what I'm doing."

They laughed again.

"I love your eyes," Jonathan said. "I'm going to call you Brown Eyes."

"Thanks. That's so sweet."

They both fell asleep.

In the morning, Zoe took Jonathan to the airport.

"Hey, sorry about that comment. It really did feel good to have sex with you. You know, if you don't come to this school, visit me from time to time. Okay?"

"Okay, Brown Eyes."

On the flight back to New York, he got an upgrade to first class. Jonathan thought about the money and how his life had changed. He also thought about his family, Nina, and the olive oil company.

After a few drinks, he murmured to himself, "Now we have a way out."

ELEVEN

With graduation day approaching, Jonathan spent hours working on his salutatorian speech. He had received this honor based on having the second-highest grade point average in the entire graduating class, in addition to winning numerous science awards. He had also been elected to the New York State All-Star Football Team.

The Springfield Gardens Preparatory High School administrators had wanted him to make the salutatorian speech. They told him to talk about growth, a positive outlook toward the future, and thankfulness. Jonathan would be the first African American to hold this honor.

The valedictorian was Linda. Jonathan believed that he should have been the valedictorian, but Linda beat him out by .01 percent points: he had a 3.98, and she had a 3.99 grade point average.

Linda Ma Ming-Chu was from Hong Kong. She had shiny black waist-length hair and wonderful deep, sensitive black eyes. She didn't smile much. She acted shy and very serene. She always talked about the importance of faithfulness and loyalty, but she was a tiger. She would rip out your throat if you pushed her too far. Jonathan and Linda were fierce competitors. Although she acted as if she didn't care about Jonathan, she truly trusted him.

They had worked long hours together on their science project. They were also having sex during breaks between classes and on all of their late nights, preparing for the National Science Fair. They won the Junior National Medal of Science and shared the prize. They devised a system to carry electricity using sound waves. Jonathan and Linda were able to power a small building by using only sound waves. Although it was a great idea, the U.S. Energy Commission shut it down, saying it was a "cheap trick." Yet Jonathan and Linda knew that if they could have marketed their project, electric companies around the world would have lost millions or maybe billions of dollars. So, they didn't pursue it. Nevertheless, their project put the school on the map and brought in a lot of new grant funding for the school.

Around eleven o'clock one night, Nina was out with her friends and Jonathan lay on the bed, resting.

The phone rang. "It's me."

"Linda?"

"Can you come over?"

"Are you crazy? Your father would kill me."

"I need you."

Her sobs melted his heart.

"I'm in trouble," Linda cried.

Jonathan dressed and got his gun, then called Thunder and Lightning, and they walked over to her house. It took about ten minutes to get there. He didn't feel anxious being on the street that late, because he knew his dogs would kill anyone on command who approached him.

Linda met him at the door. Without saying a word, she let him and the dogs into the house. She grabbed his hand, and they went upstairs. The dogs followed.

Jonathan was thinking sex, but when she opened the door to her bedroom, he saw two severely injured men lying on the floor, half-naked in a lake of blood. One of the men, Linda explained, was her father. The second was his friend.

Jonathan looked around to assess the damage. He walked over to the father and checked his pulse. Though still alive, the man was moaning and holding his chest. He said to Jonathan, "Help me, please."

"Go downstairs," Jonathan told his dogs. "Stay, don't move."

Jonathan had seen the face of death many times, and the words of a dying coward were always the same: *I don't want to die.* The other man wasn't talking, though he was still alive.

Jonathan grabbed Linda's arm and asked her again, "What happened here?"

"They came into my bedroom," she said. "I was on the bed reading. and my father's friend grabbed my arms and pinned me down on the bed and raped me, while my father just stood there looking at him. It hurt so bad. Then my father took his turn. They treated me like dirt. I'd just had enough of the rapes. This time I was ready."

"Why didn't you tell me this before?"

"I was so scared. Plus, they told me they would kill me if I ever said a word."

"Fuck me! This is a real fucking mess."

"Please . . . help me."

"Where is the knife?"

She showed him the bloody knife she'd taken from her father's collection. He took it from her.

Jonathan didn't know much about knives, but he recognized this one. It was a military combat weapon used in close-quarters combat. His Uncle Duke had one. Linda had really slashed them up. They were both totally incapacitated. It was a gory mess.

The man said it again: "Please help."

"Shut the fuck up!"

The man grabbed Jonathan's leg. Enraged, Jonathan plunged the knife into his stomach and said, "I told you to shut the fuck up!"

"What are we going to do?"

"We should call 911," Jonathan suggested.

"No!" Linda said. "If we call 911, my life is over."

"Where's your mother?"

"She's in Hong Kong, visiting her sick mother. Jonathan, if you can, please help me, because I don't know what to do. I can't leave them here. Please help me!"

Jonathan knew exactly what to do. He wasn't sure whether he trusted Linda, but he was here and couldn't leave her. *If I help her and she tells on me, I will kill her and her mother.*

He grabbed his gun and put on the silencer. He handed the gun to Linda.

"You have to shoot them," Jonathan said. "They have to die, or they are going come back and kill you and now me. This is the way it has to be. It's the only way."

"I can't."

He positioned himself behind her and pressed his body against hers. He could feel her heartbeat racing, along with her panicked breathing.

He put his left hand on her stomach and slowly, sensually, rubbed her belly. "Take a deep breath and relax. Follow my breathing."

Linda relaxed, and he rubbed her chest. She leaned her head back, and he kissed her.

"I could fuck you right now," she said.

"Shit, I am so ready."

As her breathing slowed, she spun around and kissed him again. They gazed into each other's eyes. For a moment, it was an instant feeling of affection, but it quickly turned to lust.

He turned her around and ever so gently put the gun in her hand. He held her soft hand in his. They pointed the gun at the father's heart.

Jonathan whispered, "Two in the heart and one in the head. Now shoot those motherfuckers!"

She looked up at Jonathan and he nodded. Together, they pulled the trigger multiple times, shooting both men.

They wrapped the bodies in plastic bags and put them in the trunk of the father's car. Linda went back up to the room and got some cleaning supplies and bleach.

"Are you trying to send us to prison?"

"What?"

"Bleach! The crime scene investigators will uncover this in a second."

"I don't understand."

"Luminol, the Kastle-Meyer Color test, and Fluorescein will detect not only the blood, but also bleach. Get me some white vinegar and hydrogen peroxide. They'll break down the proteins and iron ions found in blood."

"So, no proteins and iron ions, no detection of blood. You're smart. You're making me hot."

"Focus. I get it, you so horny."

They both laughed.

"There will be time for that later," Jonathan said.

They scrubbed the room down for about an hour. Jonathan felt comfortable that they'd cleaned up all of the blood, but for good measure, he scrubbed again. Neither of them said a word. Linda followed Jonathan as if they had been hanging out all of their lives.

They both showered, and Jonathan took her bloody nightgown into the basement and burned it in a pail.

They drove to a city no-parking zone. Jonathan figured that the police would tow the car, and they might not find the bodies for months. Jonathan and Linda cleaned the car of fingerprints, wiped off the keys, and put them in the trunk of the car. He took her home.

"I know you're not okay, but this is the choice we made. It's the world we live in. You can't say a word, or we'll both go to prison."

She looked at Jonathan. "I'm all in."

"If the police come, just say, I don't know."

"Okay."

"Say it."

"I don't know."

"Good. Get some rest."

"Hey, Jonathan, you know I love you, right?"

"I know."

"Come in for a few."

They had sex, and then Jonathan and his dogs left.

With graduation only a few days away, Jonathan was having problems sleeping. His mind was consumed by what he wanted to do with his life.

I'm sixteen years old, and I have more than 550 million dollars in the bank. I'm financially set for the rest of my life. I need to put my life in some type of order. It seems to be falling apart. I don't know if I can hold on. I feel so sad and alone. It's a struggle to stay alive for just one more second. I'm in some kind of aggressive interpersonal war. All I think about is life and death, and these thoughts are killing me. They're becoming my own weapons of mass destruction. With some people, I don't care whether they live or die. I have no sympathy for anyone who tries to hurt me. I'm selfish. One thing I've learned is that nobody gives a fuck about me.

I want to cry, but there's a brick wall around my heart. It's keeping me from feeling guilt. I want someone to show me how I can be free.

I don't think every problem can be solved by a peaceful resolution. Some people can't just sit down in a group and discuss their feelings. But I can't overcome every difficulty with physical force. I can't just pick up my weapon and kill each person, one by one, or plan a mass murder to get to one person. But sometimes-physical force is necessary, and casualties of war are acceptable. It's inevitable if I want peace.

"You need to stop thinking and come to bed," Nina said. "You haven't slept in days."

"Thanks, Trixie, but I can't sleep."

"You need to."

"Trixie, do you think that evil people exist in this world?"

"Baby, they're all over. Now come and hold me, so we can sleep."

"I can't sleep."

"Okay, let have sex, and I'll put your ass to sleep."

"Trixie."

"Yes."

"Nothing."

Jonathan wrapped his arms around her and kissed her. After they made love, he fell asleep.

On the morning of graduation, Jonathan woke up feeling excited and proud of himself. He dressed in a blue suit, a white shirt, a red tie, and black shoes. Nina wore a navy blue pants suit.

He walked into the kitchen, where the usual stuff was going on. Tommy and Rico sat at the table, playing cards, and Anna looked drunk out of her mind. Frankie J was talking a whole bunch of nothing. His sisters sat around, sorting cocaine, and Judy was in the kitchen. About twenty-five other people lounged around the house, because it was bonus day.

"Look at the asshole," Judy said.

Jonathan had a lot on his mind. "I'm not in the mood for your shit today."

"I don't care about you. I will blow your fucking brains out."

"No wonder you don't have a man, talking like that."

Judy pulled out a gun, and Jonathan recognized the Glock.

"Do what you like. I don't have time for it today. Nice Glock 35. Love that Crimson Trace Laser grip. Such a powerful handgun for a weak-minded bitch. You need to clean that more often."

"Boy, you don't know shit. You will, wait till you get back. We're going to fuck up you and your dumb-ass wife, Nina. A trip to the hospital for the both of you. We'll see how tough you really are."

He moved closer to Judy and whispered, "Listen, I don't feel sorry for you, and I don't care what you think about or what you might do to me. I just don't care anymore. So do what you have to, because I don't fucking care anymore."

For the first time in his life, Judy didn't respond. She just stood there.

Jonathan walked over to Tommy and Rico. "Do you want to come to my graduation?"

"Sorry, kid, not today."

Well, it's only happening today, Jonathan thought, disappointed. He really wanted them to come. He liked Tommy and Rico and didn't want anything bad to happen to them.

Tommy walked Jonathan to the door and handed him some money.

"Here, this is for you. You start working tonight, so don't drink too much. This will be the last time I give you money, since you'll be working and making more than I'd be able to give you. I trust that you won't say a thing. *Capire*?"

"*Capire*. Listen, I would die first."

"You're a good kid, but your Italian sucks."

They both laughed.

Jonathan and Nina walked to the car, and Nina took the wheel. While driving, she put on the rest of her makeup. Jonathan closed his eyes for a second.

"Hey, are you okay?" Nina asked.

"I'm good."

"No pressure, but you have a promise to keep."

"I've got it taken care of. We'll be fine."

"Love you."

"Love you, too!"

"Shit, Jonathan, I forgot to tell you, Judy's with child."

"What!?"

They pulled up to the school. Though curious, Jonathan didn't have time to hear any more details about this bombshell.

The graduation ceremony was being held outdoors, and Jonathan joined his classmates. He saw all of his friends and even Renee. Tyrone was there to support Sharon.

Jonathan paused for a second to reflect on what he'd had to do to get to this point. He even thought about Darrell and wondered where he'd ended up.

As the ceremony progressed, Principal Roles announced that Jonathan would be the next person to speak.

Jonathan stood up, and the crowd applauded. A few younger classmates whistled and yelled.

"Good morning to the administration, faculty, parents, family and friends, and fellow classmates of Springfield Gardens Preparatory High School, the fighting Eagles. Welcome to the fifty-first commencement ceremony.

"Four years ago, our class met for the first time in the auditorium, and who would have thought that there were so many raw intelligent individuals in one room, and that we would mature into the strong individuals we are today?

"Many people think this is our crossroads, but I say no. Future greatness is ours; all we have to do is stay on the road that has been paved for us. Fortunately, if the road runs short, we have the ability and the intelligence to build a new one. If there is a mountain in our way, we will go through it, around it, or over it, because even in difficult times, even in times of adversity, we will not be cheated from success. No matter how low we may appear, we will always strive for excellence.

"I hope that we now know and realize we are the class that will positively usher in the new millennium. This world has stopped creating new technology. We are falling behind, and as of this day, it stops now."

The crowd cheered.

"Today is our most significant life-altering achievement. The success that every person here attained in the last four years can be measured not only by our over-filled trophy case, but by the number of us who have full scholarships to top colleges.

"Today we completed a long and difficult task. We have worked for this moment. Through our determination, perseverance, and sacrifice, we will become the true leaders of this country.

"Our talents will make a positive impact on the financial markets. Because of our exceptional skills, Fortune 500 companies will break down doors to hire us.

"As we leave this place, Springfield Preparatory High School, we are pebbles being thrown in the ocean, which will cause a ripple effect. When we return, we will bring a tsunami of change that will revitalize this world.

"I hope that this is the day we realize that we are Eagles. This is our destiny, and we hold it in the palms of our hands. As we embark on the rest of our lives, I urge you to be all that has been given to you. Because we are the future.

"We are the future lawyers who will defend the Constitution of the United States of America.

"We are the future Joint Chiefs of Staff who will protect and defend the U.S. Constitution and laws against all enemies, foreign and domestic.

"We are Eagles."

Jonathan's voice slowed down as if he were a Southern Baptist minister. People in the audience rose to their feet, one by one, in support.

"We are the future doctors who will provide affordable health care.

"We are the future medical researchers who will discover a cure for AIDS and a cure for all cancers, which have taken so many lives.

"We are Eagles."

The crowd applauded.

"We are the future civil rights leaders who will sign into law the right for people to marry whomever they love, without shame. No one in the United States of America will have to hide in the closet anymore, because we are the future, we are Eagles."

Most of the crowd rose to their feet, chanting, "We are Eagles!" louder and louder.

Jonathan knew he had to stop, so he closed the book holding his notes and turned to go back to his seat. Principal Roles tried to get the crowd under control.

Senator Jacob K. Kavits walked over to Jonathan and said, "When you finish college, come see me. You might have a future in politics."

Jonathan nodded. When he walked past Linda, he whispered, "I love you." She smiled.

After the ceremony, he hugged Nina and Renee. Linda embraced him and said, "Thank you for everything you've done for me."

Linda's mother smiled at him, and he turned and walked away.

TWELVE

Jonathan, Nina, and Renee planned to have an early dinner after the graduation ceremony. He and Nina walked to the car and waited for Renee. Jonathan turned on soft music and closed his eyes to reflect on what had happened two days ago.

He had been staring at himself in the bathroom mirror, admiring his physique. In the last few years, he had shot up from 4 feet, 5 inches, and 60 pounds to 6 feet and 190 pounds of muscle.

You're a good-looking son of a bitch, he told himself.

He heard a noise in his bedroom and put his ear to the bathroom door. He recognized Frankie's voice and started to panic, because his family never came into his room.

He opened the door to see Frankie J, Judy, Tommy, Rico, and Gail, all staring at his nude body.

"Now what?" Jonathan asked.

"I'm so sorry, kid," Tommy said.

"Shit! Please, no, Frankie, I didn't do anything wrong. I'm just going to graduation, and I'll be working for you in two days. I'm begging you, please don't hit me."

"I'm the king of the free world," Frankie said. "You're nothing but a fucking slave."

Tommy held Jonathan from behind, while Rico repeatedly punched him in the stomach. Rico dealt each crushing blow with a mischievous smile. The powerful jabs were ten times worse than the last beating, because Rico wore brass knuckles. Jonathan could taste the blood flowing out of his mouth. It seemed like he was being beaten forever.

"Please, God, help me!" Jonathan cried.

"I'm your savior, you pray to me," Frankie said.

"Frankie, please, I didn't do anything wrong."

"You being alive is wrong. I don't trust you. You're trouble. I haven't put my finger on it yet, but there will come a time when I'll put you down. I will be the one to kill you."

"I don't understand."

"This is my insurance policy. If you ever cross me, I will torture you and Nina for the rest of your fucking lives. Your life is now in my hands."

Judy took some of his clothes, cut them with her knife, and then did the unthinkable. She looked at Jonathan and walked over to the puppies. She picked up Ginger and vigorously shook the pup up and down and side to side. Ginger's brother Mr. Moe got angry, and before Jonathan could stop him, he bit Judy on the leg.

Judy pulled a gun out of her purse and shot Ginger and Mr. Moe each twice in the head.

"Fuck you, Judy!" Jonathan screamed. "You're a fucking cunt bitch. How fucking could you? Run, Thunder, run!"

The dogs ran out of the room.

"Fuck me, you don't have the balls." She kicked him between his legs.

Tommy let him go, and Frankie laughed.

Judy told everyone to move out of the way. When Jonathan tried to stand up, Judy shot 20,000 volts from her Taser into his chest. All he could do was lie on the ground, soaking in his own urine, as Judy and Gail kicked him a few more times.

"While you sit in your own piss," Frankie said, "think about the effects of my power. I'm in control of your life, and I did this to you. I should just kill you now to get it over with."

Lying on the floor, Jonathan thought, *I could run away to another state, but I could never leave Nina, because Frankie J would torture her until she told him where I was hiding. I don't want a life on the run or a life without Nina.*

There was never a right or a wrong answer, but when it came to Nina, everything was clear. He knew what he had to do.

To kill drug dealers for raping Nina was one thing, to kill someone for trying to hurt him was different, but to kill your whole family—it was crazy.

A wave of panic swept through his mind. It was obvious that he couldn't simply wound these people. To send a strong message, he would have to kill everyone in the family. After debating with himself, he just knew. *I don't think killing is right, but for my peace of mind and Nina's, they will have to die. Kill them all. I'm not going to submit to Frankie's will; there is no need to. I believe I have the upper hand. They threatened me, and I know they will kill me at some point.*

Kill them all. It became his mantra, a chant for his survival.

There may be no other way. I must kill to stay alive, because if I stop killing, I will die. Kill them all, save myself! He wondered, *Do I have to be a killer to be truly free?*

Nina tapped him on the leg. "Hey, wake up. Renee's here."

"Not asleep. I'm just thinking." He turned the key in the ignition and started driving back toward the house.

"That was a good speech," Renee said from the backseat.

Nina playfully squeezed his leg and said with pride, "That's my baby."

"So, Jonathan, what's next for you?"

"We're going to Disneyland," he said.

They all laughed.

"Well, don't be coy."

"We're going to Tuskegee in Alabama. I'll also be taking courses at New York University in international business for my master's degree."

"Wonderful. Very nice," Renee said.

"What?" Nina asked.

"We're going to Alabama."

Nina hung her head and muttered to Jonathan, "I don't understand. How? What about tonight? We have to start working for Frankie."

Renee leaned forward and playfully whispered, "What are we talking about?"

"Nothing," Jonathan said. "It's not important."

"It's really important, Jonathan. How the fuck can you say we're going to Alabama? You know that we'll be working tonight."

"Nina, what's wrong?" Renee asked.

"Well, Mister over here is feeding me enormous amounts of bullshit. Maybe he can explain how we're going to get out of working for Frankie. And don't lie to me."

"Please stop, Nina!"

"Fuck you, Jonathan! Just go fuck yourself."

Enraged, Jonathan pulled the car over and jumped out. He ran to the passenger's side, opened the door, and yanked Nina out of the car.

"What the fuck are you going to do? You're a fucking liar!" Nina shouted. "What! You think you're a man now?"

With her dark, piercing eyes, Nina was in attack mode. She stared at Jonathan and frowned. She tried to hit him, but he blocked her slap with his left hand. In one smooth motion, he grabbed her neck with his right hand.

"Do you have a death wish?" Jonathan screamed. "What's wrong with you? I keep asking you, and you're telling me nothing."

Jonathan squeezed tighter and thought about what he was going to do to his family.

The day before graduation, he had decided that the best way to get all of them was to create an implosion through the sequential elimination of structural support and to plant enough explosives to eliminate the critical vertical structure. He had about twenty blocks of C-4 left over. He'd attached the detonator cords and the timers. He'd made a double master release button, so that they would go off simultaneously. He'd placed five C-4 blocks on the 500-gallon oil tank, six blocks on the natural gas pipeline, and five blocks in the chimney. He put the remaining four blocks on the load-bearing beams in the basement to ensure that the house would collapse.

Renee jumped out of the car, yelling, "Let her go!"

Nina's face had turned beet red. "Let me go. You're acting just like your father, you bastard."

Hearing those words come from the only lady he truly loved ripped his heart apart. It pained him to the point that he wanted to cry. He was sorry he'd hurt Nina, and he never wanted to be compared to his father.

"I said, let her go now, Jonathan," Renee repeated.

Jonathan released his grip on Nina's neck. "So, tell me what's up with you."

"You're really a fucking asshole," Nina said.

"I'm so sorry."

"Sorry! Fuck you Jonathan. You hurt me."

"Forgive me."

Nina pushed Jonathan away, and Renee snatched Jonathan's hand as they walked back to the car.

"Listen, she's going through a lot."

"Like what?"

"She has cancer."

"I didn't know."

"Money's a problem. She's been getting treatment at South Jamaica Queens County Clinic. Not the best place to get cured of breast cancer."

"Why didn't she tell me?"

"She wanted to, but she didn't want to put any more pressure on you."

"Okay, we have to get her the best, and you will help me, please."

"Yes, I will. Jonathan, you're a good man. I heard what Nina said, and I know she didn't mean it, but I don't care how furious she makes you, never put your hands on her again. That's the lady you love."

"I understand."

"You promise."

"I promise. I'll get you the money for treatments. I'll set up a checking account for her."

As Jonathan and Renee approached the car, Nina was leaning against the door with her arms crossed, biting her lower lip.

Jonathan walked over and whispered, "I'm sorry." He smiled. "You're so cute when you're mad."

"Asshole." She pushed him away. "Jonathan, I don't want to die."

"I'll do what I can to get you the best medical care in the world. I'm really sorry." He tried to kiss her, and she turned away.

"Hold up, I know you're not trying to get some pussy after choking me out. What the fuck? Were you trying to kill me?" She laughed. "I love you, but I hate you right now."

"I hurt you, so forgive me." He kissed her and thought, *There is no such thing as "trying" when I get ready to kill someone. That's the sad truth.*

Nina and Jonathan hugged, then Renee stepped in for a group hug. Nina got into the backseat with Renee and adjusted her makeup. As Jonathan drove toward the house, Nina and Renee stayed in the back, drinking rum and smoking weed.

Now Jonathan could see the house about two blocks away.

He closed his eyes for a second, reached into his pocket, and pressed a red button. He opened his eyes and heard a loud bang, then saw a cloud of smoke.

He was sad that he had to kill Tommy. Tommy had been good to him, but it was done. *Kill them and let them all die, and they shall burn.*

"What about Sharon? Is she going to Boston University?" Jonathan asked.

"Yes. The problem is that Tyrone will be going with her. He follows that poor child around like a puppy. I know he's dragging my daughter down. I tried talking to her, but she won't listen."

"Tyrone is bad news," Nina said. "That is a corrupt motherfucker. He's just like his brother Trey."

"Nina!" Renee said.

"What? Sure, I'm glad that the bastard Trey is dead."

"Wow, Nina, please tell us how you really feel."

"I don't care about that family. As far as I'm concerned, when it comes to him and his family, I will become so fucking inappropriate. Trey got exactly what he deserved."

"Okay, Nina, enough," Renee said. "Let's focus on having a good day."

"So, Jonathan, are you gonna keep changing the subject on me or what?" Nina said.

"I got you. I really do. It's going to be okay," Jonathan reassured her. "Money is not a problem."

"My type of man," Renee said. "Where are we going to eat? I'm hungry."

Jonathan responded, "I have a place."

As he turned onto Lincoln Drive, Jonathan could see smoke billowing in the sky. He saw firefighters, the police, and EMTs.

He, Nina, and Renee jumped out of the car and ran toward the house.

"What's going on?" Nina asked Jonathan.

"Let me see."

Jonathan approached a police officer. "I'm the son, and these are my sisters," pointing to Nina and Renee.

The officer lifted the yellow tape and let them through.

"Excuse me, I heard you're the son," said one of the EMTs. "Your father has third-degree burns over eighty percent of his body, and we believe he has internal bleeding. We're trying to stabilize him, before we take him to the hospital. Come with me."

Jonathan climbed into the cabin of the ambulance. He saw other EMTs working on his father. Frankie J had a neck collar on, and his arms were tied down. The left side of his face was burned beyond recognition. His face was leathery looking. He smelled like sour rotting meat. It was so pungent and overpowering, Jonathan could almost taste it. The smell of burning flesh was nauseating. He turned his head away to get control of himself.

He kneeled by his father's side and said, "Frankie."

"Some motherfucker is trying to kill me. While I'm in the hospital, find out who did this to me." Frankie J turned to the EMTs and ordered them to leave.

Jonathan looked at his father as if he'd lost his mind but didn't say anything.

"Is everyone okay?"

These were the first civilized words his father had ever said to Jonathan.

"I don't know. I'll go and find out."

As Jonathan started to get up to leave, Frankie J grabbed his arm and said, "Look under the doghouse and get that bag. Hold it for me."

"Okay."

Jonathan stood up, then stopped and said, "You were right, Frankie. I'm trouble. You should have killed me in the bathroom two days ago. I wish someone had told you about me."

"What?" Frankie was puzzled.

"I wish someone had told you how dangerous I am."

"What?"

"As you journey to eternal damnation, I want you to know that you were never a father to me. After you're gone, nobody will remember you and nobody will care."

"Fuck you!"

"One more thing: I did this to you. I'm in control of my life and I destroyed yours, so Frankie, king of the free world, as you lie there with your burned-up body, my parting words to you are, have a safe trip, motherfucker!"

"Trip?"

Jonathan stuck his head outside the ambulance and looked around. Everything was in a state of confusion, with people running around. Nobody was watching Frankie.

With one quick move, Jonathan got Frankie in a chokehold.

Frankie stared helplessly into Jonathan's eyes, as Jonathan had looked at Frankie many times in the past. Now it was Frankie who had no power. Jonathan wished that just once Frankie had showed him mercy, but all Frankie ever did was physically punish him.

Jonathan whispered, *"Dite a Dio ho detto ciao* ("Tell God I said hi")."

He twisted his father's neck and heard a loud snap that sounded like a dry tree branch. He adjusted Frankie's head and walked out of the ambulance with renewed confidence. He told himself, *It was time for those bastards to go. I feel as if I've been liberated from the forces holding me down. I'm free.*

Jonathan walked over to Nina and Renee. "Frankie's dead."

There were forty-three people in the house, all presumed dead. The house where Jonathan had lived was a smoky pile of rubble. Debris lay everywhere.

When the 105th Precinct Police Department personnel found out that Tommy and Rico had been killed, they showed up, too. Jonathan heard they were calling this a gas leak for now.

He lowered his head and slowly walked to the backyard. He let the dogs out of their pen. Because of its location, they had never been in any danger. He lifted the dogs' house and checked for any trip wires or traps. He found the bag and pulled it out. When he looked inside, he saw a lot of cash, maybe $700,000.

As Jonathan walked to the front of the house, he heard a faint sound, someone crying for help. He moved a few pieces of wood and metal sheets of wreckage and saw Judy.

"Help me, please."

"Shit!"

Jonathan put the bag over his shoulder and pulled Judy out. He carried her to the front of the house, with her head buried in his chest. He wasn't thinking about what to do next. He could have killed her with no problem, but he handed her over to the EMTs, and they took her to Jamaica Hospital.

He gave the bag to Nina.

Thunder, Lightning, and their puppies ran to the front of the house and sat a few feet away, waiting for a command from Jonathan.

After about an hour, Jonathan took his dogs to Renee's house. He, Nina, and Renee then headed toward Jamaica Hospital.

"I don't understand," Nina said.

"What don't you understand, Nina?" Jonathan asked.

"How could this happen? One moment in time you're alive and the next you're dead."

"This is some shit," Renee said. "I need a drink."

"Yes, some shit, but more of an opportunity," Jonathan said.

There was an awkward silence.

Nina said, "You know, Jonathan, you and I have got to talk."

When they arrived at Jamaica Hospital, they went to the Intensive Care Unit.

The doctor said, "She was very lucky to be alive. She lost the baby, but she will be okay and will be released in the morning."

"Thank you, Doctor."

Jonathan opened the curtain and saw Judy lying in bed. With her eyes closed, she looked almost angelic. Yet Jonathan knew she was no saint. In his mind, there were no combinations of words that he could use to answer the question why hadn't he killed this lady?

Jonathan, Nina, and Renee stood by Judy's bedside in the ICU, watching her. There were no tears lost, but Jonathan felt sad for the unborn child.

"Judy, you're awake."

"Hey, Jonathan. Hi, Nina. Sorry, I don't know your name."

Jonathan introduced Renee.

Judy looked at the women. "Can you let me have a word with my brother for a few?"

"No problem," Nina said sarcastically. She and Renee left the room.

"I'm sorry about your baby. I think you would have been a good mother."

"You're a liar."

They both laughed.

"I know you hate me. Why are you being so kind to me? You could have left me there to die, you know."

"It never crossed my mind."

"Sure, right." She smiled.

Judy smiling was an act he had never seen before. He was not impressed. It was too late; his heart was hardened.

"Judy, maybe we could try to start over."

She paused and then said, "Let's try to."

"Until we figure this out, all we have is each other."

"Maybe someone is trying to kill us."

"I don't know. It wasn't my business, so I really just don't know."

Judy grabbed his hand and said, "Thank you."

"So, you do have a soul after all."

They both laughed. Jonathan felt grossed out, looking at her, and wondered to himself whether this would ever work.

"Do you know what happened?" Jonathan asked.

"I was standing in the backyard, taking out some garbage, and first I heard a loud pop, then I saw a flash and an explosion, and within seconds the house was gone. The next thing I remember, you were picking me up."

"Just to let you know that before Frankie died, he gave me some cash. It's yours when you get out tomorrow."

"Really?" She looked up at Jonathan smiled. "You're not a bad guy, after all."

He sat down and closed his eyes. Judy went to sleep.

Jonathan heard her snoring and opened his eyes. He stared at Judy, fantasizing that he could put a pillow over her face to cut off her air supply. He visualized life leaving her body and her feet and legs jerking around as if she were doing a tribal war dance, until she was gone.

But he told himself there had been enough death for one day. He finally realized, *I'm a killer without a conscience. I've killed many people in my short life. I've killed women and children. I've killed some of my sisters. I killed my father, and I can no longer rationalize my actions, but how can I allow Judy to live after she hurt my dogs and me? How can she be so hateful to her own family?*

Renee and Nina came back into the room.

"What's up?" Jonathan asked

"Let's go and get some drinks," Renee said.

Jonathan told Judy that they'd pick her up when she was ready. As they left, two men identified themselves as detectives and asked Jonathan to follow them to a small conference room. They all sat down.

"My name is Detective Wright, and this is Detective Gumbs. We just need to ask you some questions about today's events."

"Okay."

"I want you to tell the truth. I'm here to help you. You believe that, don't you?"

"I don't know you. Why do you think I need help?" Jonathan asked.

"Obviously, you need a friend," Detective Gumbs said.

"I have friends."

"Smartass. Are you some sort of a comedian?" Detective Gumbs asked.

Jonathan thought that these guys were assholes, but he knew he had to be careful not to tip his hand. They were smart assholes. "Do I need a lawyer?"

"Why? You did something wrong?"

"I'll call someone."

"No, no," Detective Wright said. "We're just going to ask some questions. Okay?"

"Fine."

"I don't like you," Detective Gumbs said.

Jonathan hung his head and said, "I lost my whole family, and I'm so sad."

There was an awkward silence.

"Gumbs, leave the kid alone."

"Whatever," Detective Gumbs said.

"Where were you when this happened?" Detective Wright asked.

"I was at my graduation."

"Can anybody verify this?"

"You can call Springfield High School, if you like."

"Okay. Do you know what happened?" Detective Wright asked.

Jonathan remembered that he told Linda to say, "I don't know," if the cops asked her any questions about her father. Jonathan paused for a second and thought, *If I'm wise enough to counsel others, then I should be intelligent enough to accept my own guidance, and that will be sufficient to lead me directly out of trouble.*

"I don't know."

"What do you mean, you don't know?" Detective Gumbs asked.

Jonathan wanted to tell him to go fuck himself, but he was able to muster up some tears. "I don't know what happened." His voice sounded like an innocent little boy's.

"It's okay. Do you want some water?" Detective Wright asked.

"No. Thank you."

"Did you know that your father was conducting gang activities?"

"I didn't know."

Detective Wright gave Jonathan a list of names and asked whether he knew any of them.

Jonathan looked at the list and said, "No."

"Are you sure you didn't know them?" Detective Gumbs asked.

"Yes, I'm sure." Jonathan knew there was a time to lie and a time to tell the truth. "My father pushed me to go to college. He always pushed education on me. And that's how I will honor his memory, by going to college."

"Okay, fair enough. Why were there so many people in the house early in the morning?"

"I don't know."

The detectives didn't say a word, and Jonathan knew that this was bullshit. He knew the game. The first one to talk would lose. He sat quietly.

After a few moments, Detective Wright asked, "How well did you know Tommy and Rico?"

"Tommy taught me how to drive and gave me money from time to time. They came to my football games. Rico was always with Tommy, but he never talked much."

"Did you know they were detectives?"

"Yes, I knew."

"Finally, you know something," Detective Gumbs said.

"Go easy," Detective Wright said.

"Do you know why they were at the house with your father?"

"I don't know. They were always there."

Detective Gumbs said, "So what you're telling us is that you don't know shit. You're no use to us."

"Sorry, I just don't know."

"Okay, kid, you can go. But don't leave town."

"I'm going to college, so I'm out in August."

"Where are you going?"

"To Alabama."

"Who's paying?"

"I got a football scholarship."

"Okay. Good luck, and sorry for your loss."

"Thank you."

As Jonathan walked away, Detective Gumbs said, "That little fucker knows something."

"No, he don't. He's just a kid."

Jonathan caught up with Nina and Renee.

"Why did they question you?" Nina asked. "Do they think you're a killer?"

"Shit, I'm not saying, but this is some crazy shit," Renee said.

"No problem," Jonathan said. "It was handled."

"As it should be," Nina said.

"I guess we should be sad," Renee said.

"Whatever," Nina said. "So, what the fuck is up with you and Judy?"

"Nothing, it's all part of my master plan," Jonathan said.

They laughed, and Nina took Jonathan's hand. "Come. I want to know if you had something to do with killing Frankie."

"Why?"

"I overheard the doctors say that his neck was broken."

"And what? I don't know what happened."

"Don't give me that 'I don't know' shit! Plus, you said this was an opportunity."

Jonathan paused. "Let it go."

"No. I lost my father."

"I lost Tommy, too. You know I loved that man like a father."

"I don't get it. I don't get you, the way you're acting," Nina said.

"Again, let it go."

"I see you're not being honest with me. I think you're hiding something from me."

"It's for your own good."

"Will it come back to bite us?"

"The answer is no. Look." He pulled her close. "Have fun, travel the world. I spoke to you years ago, when we were in Ohio—I said I will take care of you."

"Where did you get the money? I know you don't sell drugs."

"Stop."

"Fine, answer this—do you love me?"

"I can't imagine my world without you and Renee. Yes, I do love you."

"Did you and Judy kiss and make up?"

"Is you crazy?"

They both laughed.

They walked out of the hospital, Jonathan in the middle, holding the women's hands.

They went to a local bar and after a few drinks headed back to Renee's. Jonathan fed and cleaned off his dogs. He and Nina drove past the house and saw cops standing around, talking. Then they went to a hotel to get some sleep.

The next day Jonathan and Nina went shopping for a few things they'd lost in the fire. He called the hospital to find out when Judy was being discharged.

At the hospital, Jonathan gave Judy a bag of money and some clothes. Henry Stein, Frankie's lawyer, was also there, with the intention of settling Frankie's estate as soon as possible.

"Jonathan, the estate, with property and cash, is worth about $23 million, which is all willed to his only son, and that would be you."

Judy looked at Jonathan and saw him glance at Nina.

"Mr. Stein, I want you to know that I don't want any money from this estate," Jonathan said.

"Take that money, boy," Nina said.

"It's my decision, and I want Judy and my other sisters and their mothers to have the money."

Mr. Stein told Jonathan that his father had about $500,000 in insurance policies. He said he would make all of the funeral arrangements, and they wouldn't have to worry about anything.

Mr. Stein gave Jonathan some paperwork to review and fill out, so that he could make the necessary arrangements to have Frankie's estate transferred to Jonathan's sisters.

Judy smiled at Nina. She asked Nina and Mr. Stein to leave the room. "Look, Jonathan, I know we're not friends, and I really know you hate me, but you should think about this. That's a lot of money."

"I know it's a lot of money, but I don't want it. Plus, I'm sure Frankie didn't make it easy for them."

"You're right about that. Wow," Judy said. "I'm so very sorry for hurting you. Whatever I did, please try to forgive me. I didn't realize you were such a nice guy. It was just business."

"Just business."

Jonathan stepped out into the hallway, so Judy could get dressed.

"What the fuck is wrong with you?" Nina said.

"You asked me to take care of you, so we could make a life together. Just follow my lead."

"But—"

"But nothing! Just be a good girl and follow me. I got you all the way. Anyway, there is nothing in this world that could erase the pain that bitch caused."

"Okay, but we need to talk."

"Fine."

"I don't get it."

"You will, just relax."

"Okay, but what's up with you and Judy?"

"Are you jealous? Do think that Ms. Judy is threatening our relationship?"

"You can be a real asshole at times. And the answer is yes, I'm jealous."

"I love you. Please don't let jealousy bring us down. We worked too hard, and I refuse to let anyone come between us. I'm going to help Judy, get her set up, and then we're going to Alabama. Don't worry about money. Deal?"

"Deal."

Judy appeared at the door. "Hey, you two, I'm ready to get outta here."

She asked Jonathan to take her to a hotel and said she would hang out there until the funeral service.

While they were in the car, Judy handed Jonathan about $100,000 in cash from Frankie's bag and thanked him for all of his help.

Jonathan gave the money to Nina.

THIRTEEN

Harvey Stein, Frankie's lawyer, set up the funeral arraignments. The viewing was attended by Jonathan, Nina, Renee, Judy, and Mr. Stein. There was no funeral service or minister preaching to them or sending Frankie off to a new world. No other people attended or came to say goodbye.

When I die, Jonathan wondered, *who's going to be at my funeral service? I don't want to die alone, but my actions imprisoned me. The reality of the damage I've caused is taking an emotional toll on me. Am I evil?*

Frank J. Russo, father; Anna Maria Russo, stepmother; and Jonathan's stepsisters, Gail, Anna, Maria, Paula, Taren, and Alicia were all going to be buried at Pineland Cemetery, Queens, New York. There were eight caskets, all lined up to take the bodies to their final resting place. Jonathan hoped that their souls would be put in a fiery oven so that they burned throughout eternity, in perpetual torment.

I'm happy everyone except Judy is dead, but I'm not sure of my true feelings. I had a miserable life with my family. They were incapable of loving me. I was just a vulnerable little boy who needed the affection and nurturing of my parents. All I ever wanted was to be loved and to have the warm, understanding touch of a mother. With them out of my life, no longer will I be paralyzed with fear. That fear was turning me into a coward. I was in turmoil at every juncture of my sixteen years on this earth. I have psychological and physical scars that might never go away. But now I have an opportunity for a good life and to heal my feelings of anxiety. Did I make the correct decision to kill my family? Absolutely!

While Jonathan and Nina walked to the limo, Mr. Stein told them,

"There will be a meeting in the morning. I did everything you asked in reference to the last will and testament."

"Thank you," Jonathan said.

The next morning, Jonathan, Nina, and Judy drove into Midtown Manhattan. The law firm was in Times Square. As soon as they arrived at the office, a receptionist took them into a large conference room. Jonathan saw nothing but women sitting around the conference table.

Mr. Stein walked over to him and said, "These are your sisters."

Jonathan looked around the room at the beautiful young ladies.

Mr. Stein introduced everyone. "This is Brenda, your birth mother, and these are her children, Lisa, Kara, and Sandra."

Jonathan turned blue. He tried his best to hide his emotions.

Wow! Mother-fuck me! he thought. *I had sex with my sister.*

Tears flowed from Lisa's eyes, as she tried not to look at Jonathan. He needed all of his energy to keep his emotions in check. He glanced at Lisa and figured she was just as hurt.

Mr. Stein continued the introductions: "This is Kia, Tina, Chelsea, Jada, Diana, Joan, Melissa, Aria, Linda, and Sandra. Their mother is Karen. Everyone, this is your oldest sister, Judy, and your only brother, Jonathan."

Jonathan took his place at the head of the table. The lawyer opened a package and gave each person a copy of the last will and testament.

"Frankie gave $50,000 to each of the daughters and $100,000 to Brenda and Karen. The remainder of his estate was to go to Jonathan, which was valued at $23 million in cash and real estate."

Brenda stood up and said, "Hell, no! Will it all go to him? Why the fuck should it? This is some bullshit!"

"That's right," Lisa said. "Why should he get it all?"

Lisa was just like her big-mouthed mother. Karen's daughters didn't say a word.

"That's what Mr. Russo wanted," Mr. Stein said. "But—"

"But nothing. Fuck Jonathan. We had these kids. We need the money," Brenda said. "This is really screwed up. That's why I hate Frankie so much. Even in death, he's still fucking us over."

Jonathan stood up, and the room got quiet. "I don't want the money," he said. "I don't want anything from that person. My sisters, Karen, and my mother can have it all. The money and the property will be equally split. I trust that Mr. Stein took care of everything."

The atmosphere was extremely tense, but after that announcement, everyone calmed down. They all looked happy, with the exception of Nina. She wanted Jonathan to take the money, so they could travel the world. Yet he already had enough money to pay for college and do whatever he wanted with his life. Plus, he would get a check for $400,000 from the insurance company.

After the legal fees were paid, each person received a check for about $1 million.

Nina and Jonathan left and walked to the end of the block, where they stood outside a coffee shop.

"What the hell was that all about? Didn't you think of me?"

"We have enough money."

"Where? How are we going to live? What did you do?"

"Look! You asked me to take care of things, and I did. I got you. Just calm down, please."

"Why?"

"Because I have something better."

"Better! Like?"

"Like, stop asking so many questions."

"You really need to be careful around Judy, because she's not to be trusted."

"You think I forgot and all is forgiven? Fuck her."

"Okay, what's wrong with you? I hear it in your voice."

"I have a lot on my mind. Do you remember when I told you about that girl who beat me and forced me to have sex with her when I was ten years old?"

"Yes, I remember."

"Well, that was her in the conference room."

"No shit! Which one?"

"It's Lisa."

"Wow. You fucked your sister." She laughed.

"That's not fucking funny!"

"Sorry. You also saw her in Alabama, right?"

"Yes. My life is so fucked," Jonathan said.

"I have to take care of a few things. I'll see you later."

"Sure."

"Are you okay?" Nina asked.

"Just need some time alone."

They hugged, and Nina left Jonathan standing in front of the coffee shop.

Jonathan was never one to cry. He kept his emotions bottled up, and when he played football, all of his feelings of being unloved, even hated, and all the fights he had with his family came out on the football field.

Jonathan believed he killed only out necessity and not for revenge or anger. Yet the fact that he'd had sex with his sister took him in another emotional direction.

He didn't know what he was feeling. His stomach ached. A blank, emotionless expression swept over his face. The truth became entrenched in his mind, as he gradually realized he was a depraved individual. He wanted to die.

Sometimes the pain is too much to handle, he thought. *There are no pills in this world that can comfort me, and the only answer is to end my life. I'm just standing here trying to put my thoughts in some kind of order, because it seems like I'm falling apart. I sometimes feel that I cannot hold on. There's a war inside my mind, and I'm becoming my own weapon of mass destruction.*

I'm trying to keep breathing, but it's getting harder. I feel my heart beating faster and faster. I feel so alone. I'm struggling to stay alive, for just one more second.

Jonathan's legs got weak, his eyes blurred from tears, everything got dark, and he fell to his knees and wept, for sixteen years of pain.

FOURTEEN

Jonathan wanted to do something nice for Nina and Renee. They had been such good friends to him and played a great role in his life. He treated Nina and Renee to a thirty-day paid cruise to Europe and invited Judy and Renee's sister Jasmine to join them.

Their flight would leave from Boston to connect with the ship sailing out of Fort Lauderdale. Jonathan, Renee, and Nina drove to Boston to meet Judy and Jasmine. He took the five dogs on the road trip in his 1976 Oldsmobile Ninety-Eight, so the car was pretty crowded.

Renee thought the best place for Sharon would be at Boston University, where she could study law and be under the watchful eye of her Aunt Jasmine, because Renee didn't trust Tyrone.

Jasmine was Renee's only sister and lived in Boston. Jasmine had never married and didn't have any kids. She was credited with single-handedly infiltrating a merciless gang named the South Street Walker Boys in Oklahoma City. This ruthless gang made about $9 million a month selling drugs. When Jasmine's undercover assignment was over, she moved to Boston, where she became the first black female captain detective in Boston's police department.

Renee entered Danielsen Hall and found Sharon's dorm room. Jasmine was helping Sharon organize the room, while Tyrone watched, drinking a beer.

Judy took a walk around the campus, and Jonathan and Nina waited by the car. The dogs had their heads hanging out the open windows, anxious for something to happen.

"Are you okay?" Nina asked.

"Sure, why?"

"I'm just asking. Can I help you?"

"No. Really. I'm fine now."

"I worry about you."

"I know."

"Don't shut me out, okay?"

"I'm better. It's like I can think clearly again."

"Thank you for the trip. I really need to get away."

"Are you and Renee going to play nice with Judy?"

"Whatever."

"Anyway, I hope Sharon can get it together," Jonathan said.

"Don't worry about Sharon. She doesn't listen. I tried to talk to her about Tyrone, but she didn't want to hear it. When she's ready, she'll figure it out for herself. If not, fuck her."

"No, thank you. Been there, done that." They both laughed.

"Funny, you have a way with words when you talk about her," Nina said.

"I know. I don't like that bitch."

"I guess she'll be fine."

Jonathan handed Nina an envelope that contained $20,000 in hundreds.

"Thanks."

"Have a good time." He leaned over, gave her a kiss, and hugged her tightly. "I love you so much."

"I'll see you in Alabama. Drive carefully. Leave those nasty girls alone while you're in Tuskegee. I don't want to kick some country bitch's ass when I get there."

They both laughed.

While Judy talked to Jasmine, Tyrone walked out of the dormitory. He saw Jonathan. "Let me holla at you."

"What's up?"

"Look, we have been boys for a long time, so do you want to come and work for me?"

"No."

"No! Look, you're just a motherfucker, just trying to get by, that's all you will ever be. I want you to ride with me, so we—you, and I—can become supreme beings in the drug game. College is shit, it's about . . . where is your soul, Jonathan? What defines you? I can make you rich. Alan and Ray are down. It would be just like old times."

While Tyrone was talking, Jonathan wanted to say, "I killed your brother."

"As I remember, the old times were not good times for me, so my answer is still no."

"Seriously, you and I can make a lot of money together."

"Not me! I can't put myself out there to get killed."

"I got this."

"Famous last words of an egomaniac."

"Your loss."

"Maybe your loss," Jonathan said.

"You think you're better than me. Fuck you! I fucked your bitch, and you didn't do shit. You will always be a soft motherfucker to me."

"Whatever."

"Maybe I just might get a taste of Nina. She's a fine piece of ass."

"You watch your fucking mouth."

"Fuck you."

"You're going to die out there, but that's your choice. That's not my life, and yes, I'm better than you for that."

"So whatever you had with Sharon, get over it. You two are done. Move the fuck on. You understand me or—"

"Or fucking what!?"

Tyrone grabbed Jonathan and push him against the car. Tyrone reached for his gun, but before he could pull it out, Thunder leaped out of the car window and took hold of his arm. The dog's momentum knocked Tyrone to the ground. Jonathan jumped on top of Tyrone and slipped the gun out of his waistband.

Tyrone yelled, "Let me go!"

In a sinister voice, Jonathan said, "Just wait."

With the gun in his hand, Jonathan looked at Tyrone and said, "Next time you reach for your gun, you'd better be faster."

"Fuck you!"

Thunder held Tyrone's arm, and now Lightning sailed through the open car window, growling.

"Fuck me, really!" Jonathan said.

Jonathan held Tyrone's gun, a Desert Eagle and broke it down. He took the clip out, then pressed the spring-loaded pin, and the barrel came off. He put the parts on Tyrone's chest and ordered his dogs to stand down.

"Pussy," Jonathan said.

He turned around and saw Judy, Nina, Sharon, Renee, and Jasmine watching what had happened.

Tyrone got up and tried to put the gun back together but couldn't, so he just threw the parts into his car. Sharon rushed to his aid.

"This shit is not over!" Tyrone yelled. "Next time I'm going to kill you."

"Back at you, bitch."

Nina, Judy, and Renee joined Jonathan.

"What the hell?" Nina said.

"No problem."

"You okay?" Judy asked.

"I don't like the motherfucker," Renee said.

There's not enough money in this world for me to be on the street selling drugs, Jonathan thought. He had his heart set on going to college. He laughed to himself. *The last person who tried to stop me from going to college ended up dead.* He called the dogs and put them in the car.

Renee came over and introduced her sister to Jonathan. He took Nina's and Renee's bags to Jasmine's car, then hugged Renee and wished her a safe trip.

Renee and Jasmine both thanked Jonathan for the cruise.

Nina hugged him and said, "I love you. Thanks again."

"Anytime."

She walked over Jasmine's car.

"Hey," Judy said. "You know I was just following orders, right? It was just business."

"I know. Just business." Standing in front of Judy, Jonathan was repulsed at the sight of her. There was no such thing as business when it came to blood. He felt his white-hot hatred for her as if his body were on fire.

She'd wanted him dead a few weeks ago. Jonathan had given her a pass. As far as he was concerned, she owed him a life debt, because he'd literally spared her life. She was indebted or in some way connected to him, but Jonathan would not give her a chance to pay off the debt. He would kill her first.

"Judy, you take care of yourself. You have a second chance, so make the best of it."

"Thank you for being there for me. You did a nice job with those dogs. I'm sorry again, about the puppy thing."

He had Thunder, Lightning, King Ren, Shadow, and Allie with him. He had not forgotten what Judy did to his dogs. She attempted to hug him, but he turned and walked away.

Jonathan opened the car door, and the dogs jumped out. He let them run for a few minutes. It would be a challenge driving from Boston to Tuskegee, Alabama, with five dogs—roughly a twenty-three-hour drive.

FIFTEEN

Around 8:30 in the evening, as Jonathan drove on Interstate 95 headed south, he merged onto Interstate 295 South. He somehow got turned around and ended up on Route 152 going toward Attleboro, Massachusetts. He realized his error and that he was on the wrong highway, so he pulled the car over and let the dogs run.

He aimed his flashlight at the map, trying to find his way back to the correct highway. A white pickup truck sped past. He didn't pay any attention to it, but when he looked up again, its brake lights were lit.

The truck slowly backed up and pulled in behind Jonathan's car. Jonathan folded his map and decided to get back on Interstate 95 South. Five white guys jumped out of the pickup truck.

"You need help? Are you lost or something?"

"No, thank you. I'm good."

"Nice ride."

"Thanks."

The white teenager looked at Jonathan with disgust. He approached Jonathan and said, "I really like this car."

"Thanks again."

"You shouldn't be alone on this road."

"Why?"

"Why? Because these are my roads, and you have to pay tax."

"How do you know I'm alone, and why do I have to pay you a tax?" Jonathan asked.

"What did you say to me?"

Another of his friends said, "Come on, let's go."

"Anyway, I got lost," Jonathan said. "Now I'm on my way."

"Where you headed?"

"Alabama," Jonathan said.

"Alabama, what the fuck is in Alabama?"

"Sorry?"

"You heard me—ass wipe."

"Hey, Jeff, leave him. Let's go."

"Fuck off, Bobby. The boy looks like he got money."

"What does a person look like who has money?" Jonathan paused for a second and said, "Look! I don't want any trouble."

"Too late for that. The only way you're leaving here is walking."

Jonathan prayed to God that they would just get in the truck and go away. He'd hoped a state trooper would come by and help, but he realized he was on his own once again.

Jonathan allowed them to continue hassling him without calling his dogs, only because he didn't know how the puppies would react. He wanted to see how far the boys were willing to go before it would be too late to stop Jonathan's rampage of death.

He knew that all bets were off when one of the guys went back to the truck and pulled out a baseball bat and a lead pipe.

One more time, Jonathan made a passionate appeal for them to get back in their truck and go home. "This will not go well for you guys, so please go away."

"Look around ass, there's five of us and one of you. What the fuck are you going to do?"

"Well, I won't be pleading for my life, that's for sure."

"What?"

"Last chance," Jonathan said.

"Fuck you. Kill that motherfucker."

Jonathan could see King Ren slowly coming out of the bushes. He knew Thunder and Lightning were not too far away.

One of the men drew closer. Jonathan's heart beat faster with anticipation. There might be some problems.

King Ren barked and distracted one of the guys.

Jonathan pulled out his weapon and shot two boys, with "two in the heart and one in the head." He reloaded.

Thunder and Lightning each grabbed a boy, with the help of Shadow and Ren. Jonathan commanded them to attack. One boy tried to jump into the truck, but Allie was there, waiting for him.

Jonathan heard the screams, about how sorry the boy was, but all appeals came only after Jonathan had gotten the upper hand.

They all cry the same way, when I see fear in their eyes.

Jonathan said, "Help me move your friends."

They pulled the four bodies to the side of the road and into the bushes.

"Please don't kill me," the boy said.

"Why not? I asked you to stop."

"I'm sorry. I don't want to die."

Jonathan looked around to see if anybody was coming. The young man kept begging Jonathan to spare his life.

"My father is the mayor, and he would help you."

Jonathan knew deep down in his heart that letting this boy live would be a big mistake. The boy finally offered him money, but Jonathan knew this was not about money. It was about preserving his life.

He said, "Keep your money."

"No! No! No!" the boy screamed.

Jonathan put two bullets in his heart and one in his head. He wiped the dogs off and hustled them into the car. He made his way back to Interstate 95 South and drove until he reached Kingsport, North Carolina.

He pulled onto the side of the road and let the dogs out. Leaning against the car, he stared at the sky. It was about 4:15 in the morning.

All my life, I have been running, he thought. *Not physically but emotionally. I've allowed people to hurt me and dictate how to act. I'm basically living someone else's dream. I don't want all of this death and destruction on me anymore. But I do realize that no matter how much I run or try to hide, I somehow get pulled back into this unpleasant life.*

Jonathan thought about what he'd done in Attleboro. While he contemplated his next move, it crossed his mind not to go to college, to turn around and live a dream life with his money.

Jonathan saw a North Carolina state trooper pull up behind his car. He was surprised that the cop was female. She was attractive looking, for a white woman, and had big muscles. Jonathan laughed to himself.

"Morning, sir, do you have a problem?"

"No problem, ma'am."

"What are you doing out here?"

"I'm headed to Alabama. I needed to stop and let my dogs run."

She looked around and then looked back at Jonathan. "I don't see any dogs."

"I'm going to call them, and when I do, don't be scared. There are five of them, but they're very friendly, okay?"

"Okay."

Jonathan yelled for his dogs, and they came in peace, with tails wagging.

"Wow! Nice dogs. And so well-trained."

"Thank you."

"What are their names?"

Jonathan called them, one by one: Thunder, Lightning, King Ren, Shadow, and Allie. The state trooper played with the dogs, while Jonathan slipped away to hide his gun in the glove box. He returned to see them still jumping all around her. She seemed to be having fun.

The state trooper walked around the car and instructed Jonathan to open the trunk. She looked inside, only to see dog supplies and some luggage.

"So, where you headed?"

"Going to college at Tuskegee."

"Good school. Playing ball?"

"Yes, ma'am."

"You can stop calling me ma'am."

"Okay."

Jonathan wondered how long he had to entertain her, because he wanted to get on the road and get everything set up.

"So, you're the keeper of these highways."

"Yes."

"I'm surprised to see a woman state trooper."

"Not many of us, but it's a good living. It gets lonely out here, though. You know."

"I can't imagine being out here all night by myself. What's your name?"

"Call me Sue."

"I'm Jonathan."

"Well."

"Well, what?"

She paused for a second. "Nice car. Must be a lot of work traveling with five dogs."

"Yes, it is."

"They're smart dogs."

"Yes. I trained them. They're very loyal. Do you have a dog?"

"No."

"Everyone should have a dog or a partner."

"No, it's slim pickings in these parts."

"Well, I would be happy to part with one for free, if you want."

She smiled like a little kid. "How do I know they're yours?"

"I have all of their papers and shot information."

"But I can't. You know, police policy."

"Okay, no problem."

"How old are you?

"Just turned seventeen, why?"

"Just checking. Well."

"Why—to see if I'm legal?"

They both laughed.

They exchanged numbers, and he was on the road again.

Jonathan thought, *I wish there would come a time when I could experience true happiness, not from alcohol, drugs, or sex, but true spirit-filled joy so that I can create a complete life for myself. I hope and trust my life will not be only killing and fucking.* He laughed to himself.

He kept driving until he reached South Carolina, then stopped at Joker Joe's truck stop to get food for the dogs.

Inside, he ordered some burgers. After he finished feeding the dogs, he looked up and saw several men standing at the entrance of the truck stop, watching him.

A heavyset white man approached him. "Hey, son, nice dogs."

"Thank you."

"Are they yours?"

"Yes."

Jonathan wasn't sure where this was going, so he just went along with it. There were too many people watching for him to perceive that this might be a dangerous situation.

"Are you selling?"

Jonathan believed that this was a good thing.

"No, I'm not selling, but I would be happy to give you one. I have the papers, and they're all registered with the American Kennel Club."

Jonathan gave up Allie.

Before he got back on the road, he bought *USA Today* at the newsstand and looked it over. An article described the five people he'd killed, the reporter calling the incident the "Attleboro Highway Massacre." It was the highest number of murders that had been committed in that town in years.

Jonathan didn't worry, but he did notice that further along in the news report, the writer made a comparison with the bodies found in New York, one in Springfield Park. *That would have been Sharon's father, James.* The other body was found in the trunk of a car at the New York City police impound lot. *That would have been Linda's father.* These bodies were decomposed beyond recognition. However, they were shot the same way, two bullets in the heart and one bullet in the head. The reporter wrote that the animals that mauled the two boys were the same as those that killed the police officer in Queens, New York. *Who tried to rape me,* Jonathan thought.

The Attleboro Police Department was working with the New York City Police Department. Accompanying the article were photos of Detective Wright and Detective Gumbs, the men investigating the deaths in his family.

Jonathan threw the paper away, finished his coffee, and made his way to Tuskegee, Alabama.

SIXTEEN

Tuskegee Institute was the pride of the swiftly growing South, and Jonathan felt glad to be part of its rich heritage. On arriving, he had a very busy week. He purchased a house for Nina and his dogs at 309 Barrow Street—the last house before all you could see were acres of land. It was a perfect place to hide.

Assigned to one of the oldest dormitories on campus, Jonathan stayed in Emery Three, room number four. He hung out with fourteen guys from all over the United States. Jonathan smiled to himself, thinking, *I'm glad I came here. It was a good move.*

The school considered Jonathan a second-semester sophomore, because he had taken college-level courses in high school. College classes came easily for him, and he didn't have to work as hard as the rest of the students.

The hangout was at the "ignorant bench," a place where the guys drank beer, talked sports, and made rude remarks to women. Within a few weeks, Jonathan had become a presence on campus. He was eighteen years old and 215 pounds—loved by the ladies and hated by several jealous guys.

"Hello," Jonathan said.

"Hey."

"What's your name? Where're you from?

"Bridget. I'm from a small town in Illinois called Maywood."

"I'm Jonathan Anthony Russo from New York."

"I know. I heard your family died in a fire."

Jonathan paused and tried his best not to react. "Where did you hear that?"

"Small town, we know shit about people."

"I don't like it."

"Well, you could always use it to get some sympathy pussy."

Jonathan's face tightened, and then they both laughed.

"Sorry." She rubbed his face.

"No problem. So, what's your story?"

"I'm a Golden Tiger cheerleader. I see you out there on the football field. You look good."

"Thanks. I probably won't get any playing time, because of the running back. Timothy Blake is the hometown favorite."

"He's a jerk."

"Why? Is he your boyfriend?"

"Hell, no! Do I look like the type of girl who would hang out with an asshole?"

"He looks very familiar to me. Do you know where he's from?"

"Tuskegee, I heard. He was a star at Tuskegee High School. I know he lives with his mother. But there's a rumor that he was in a bad accident and had plastic surgery."

"Interesting. I have to go to class. I'll talk to you later, okay? Where are you staying?"

"Adams Hall. Come by around six tonight."

"Later."

After football practice, Timothy Blake approached Jonathan.

"I don't like you, rookie." The locker room got quiet. "I'm the starting running back, and you're a fucking rookie. So keep your fucking mouth shut. Get me a steak sandwich from Big Kidd Sandwich Shop."

Jonathan stood up and gave Timothy a nasty look.

"What the fuck are you going to do? You gonna fight me? You getting up and looking at me like you're going to bring it. What the fuck is up? I know you, motherfucker."

"How do you expect me to get your sandwich, scoot on my ass?"

Everyone in the locker room laughed. Timothy threw some money on the floor. "Pick that shit up, and you better watch your back."

Jonathan looked at the money and said, "That's okay, I buy the first one." He paused. "Yo, Blake, go fuck yourself."

Jonathan couldn't shake the feeling that he knew Timothy. For the next few months, that's the way it was: Jonathan was Timothy's bitch. He didn't complain because he knew that was part of being a rookie.

Nina came to visit Tuskegee in November for the homecoming game.

While they lay in bed, relaxing, she said, "Do you want to hear something?"

"Sure."

"I heard that your sister Judy works for Tyrone and is making millions. She's his number two in the organization."

"She's a dumb ass."

"I remember what his brother did to me."

"Yeah, but he's dead for it. Anyway, fuck them. How do you feel?"

"I feel . . . I'm okay, just beat all the time. After the game, I have to go back to New York for more treatments. Then Renee and I are going to Canada."

"You and Renee are good friends?"

"Yeah, we are. Why, you want to fuck her?"

"Lady!"

"I see the way you look at her."

"Please stop. But . . . she has a fat ass."

"Asshole!"

"You know where I stand with you," Jonathan said.

"Love you always, but one thing I do know is that you are fucking those Southern bitches."

Jonathan paused and said, "All I need is you?"

"Fucking liar."

"Go to sleep." Jonathan thought about all of the ladies he was having sex with, but he truly loved Nina.

"Jonathan, I'm scared."

"I'm worried, too. I'll get you the best care in the world. I believe that you're going to be fine."

"I don't want to die. I don't want to leave you."

Jonathan held her, and they both fell asleep.

The night before the biggest game of the year, while Jonathan was hanging out on campus, he saw a young lady sitting on the edge of the famous Tuskegee fountain.

"Hey."

"What's up with you?" he asked.

"Nothing. Why are you talking to me? I see all those girls you're with."

"Well, I was just trying to be nice. It not like we're going to fuck later. Right?"

"Hey, you never know. I might give you some."

They both laughed.

"Are you coming to the game?" Jonathan asked.

"Maybe."

"Do you have a ticket?"

"No. Homecoming tickets are the hardest to get, if you don't have a hookup."

"Do you want a ticket?"

"Sure, what do you want for it?"

"Nothing. I'm good. I have extras. So, why were you watching me?"

"I'm a veterinary student, and I saw you with your dogs and how well behaved they are. Bring them to my office, I'd love to examine them. They're so big."

"Thank you. I'll do just that. What's your name?"

"April."

"Nice. I'd love to stay, but I have to get some sleep. Not that I'm going to be playing. But maybe we could hook up later. Here are two tickets, in case you want to bring a plus one, or you could give it away."

"You're funny. Thanks."

Jonathan nodded and walked away.

Tuskegee considered game day a big deal. Jonathan had heard that Tuskegee High School won last night, so the town was hyped up.

The next morning the sun was shining, and he felt different. He wanted to put the past behind him. Finish school, open a nonprofit organization, and maybe make some babies. He paused and then laughed to himself.

Jonathan showed up first in the locker room and jogged in place to warm up. He knew he didn't have to dress in full uniform. It bothered him that he might have to quit football, because of lack of playing time. But he still loved the game.

As the team started getting dressed for the game, the players were joking around. Jonathan didn't like the vibe in the locker room. He knew that even though Miles College was a weaker team, the mind-set in the locker room was that *"Tuskegee already won."*

The running back coach approached Jonathan. "We want you to dress for this game."

"Me?"

"You're not going to play, but we want you to be the ball boy for today. It's an honor, somewhat."

Jonathan would have to throw small toy footballs into the stands, as mementos for the fans.

"Okay, Coach."

The guys in the locker room laughed.

Timothy said, "I knew you liked balls, fuckin' fag!"

"Yeah, I do, clown. After the game, I'll let you juggle my nuts, motherfucker."

Timothy jumped out of his seat. "What the fuck did you say?"

"Knock it off!" the coach yelled.

The head coach gave a speech that would incite a riot. The team felt ready to kill anyone in its path. The football team needed a win. The Golden Tigers had two wins and three losses.

Although Jonathan carried the bag of toy footballs, he felt like part of the team as they ran down the hill into the stadium.

After the warm-ups, the national anthem, and the school song, they were ready to play.

It was the Miles College Golden Bears against the Tuskegee Institute Golden Tigers.

Jonathan felt pleased to see Nina in the stands and happy that Bridget and April had showed up, too.

With the game underway, Jonathan kept throwing toy footballs into the stands and didn't really pay attention to what happened with the game. Tuskegee was losing, 28–0.

With seven minutes left, the band warmed up for the halftime show.

Jonathan heard a very familiar sound. Timothy had been hit hard, and the sound echoed throughout the stadium. Jonathan turned looked and saw him on the ground, rolling in agony. Jonathan didn't care. In fact, he felt glad Timothy had gotten hurt.

While the doctors worked on him, the coach called Jonathan.

"I know that you don't know all the plays," the coach said. "All I want you to do is take care of my football. Whatever you see happen, don't drop the ball."

"Okay, Coach."

"Look at me, son. Take care of my ball. Go get 'em, killer!"

After some of the teammates carried Timothy off the field, Jonathan ran in.

"Hi, guys."

The quarterback said, "I'm going to hand you the ball. Don't drop the ball. Just take it and run. Got it?"

Jonathan nodded. He looked around, and in the excitement of the game, he didn't pay attention, missed the count, and almost lost the ball.

When they went back to the huddle, one of the players said, "What the fuck is wrong with you?"

"I'm sorry."

The quarterback looked at Jonathan, slapped his helmet, and said, "Wake the fuck up. Get your head out of your ass. Take the ball and run. All you have to do is run."

Jonathan nodded in agreement. A switched turned on, and he ran.

Jonathan ran all over the Golden Bears. It had taken him eight years to hear *"Go, Johnny, go! Go, go Johnny, go! Touchdown, he scores!"*

Jonathan helped his team to a 49 to 28 victory. He ran the ball 38 times, for a total of 455 yards and 7 touchdowns. It was a Southern Intercollegiate Athletic Conference record.

While Jonathan stood in the end zone next to the goalpost, he heard seventy thousand people screaming his name. With all of that cheering, nobody turned up the volume more than Nina did. He thanked God for his talents as a football player by pointing his index finger to the sky. He felt very gratified.

Jonathan finished his private celebration and turned to face the crowd. The next instant his body jerked forward and his head smacked the goalpost. He heard Nina scream, as a sharp pain shot down his spine. He hit the ground. He tried to open his eyes but couldn't. His body wouldn't respond. Then, in a haze, his eyes opened. People crowded around him, and his eyes closed again. He tried to speak, but the words would not come.

He heard a voice say, "I told you to watch your back."

The fluorescent lights harshly flickered in the bright whiteness of the hospital room. The slow beeps of a heartbeat played steadily in the background. Jonathan's mind drifted into the unknown.

SEVENTEEN

Jonathan's eyes fluttered open and took a moment to adjust.
"What . . ." He hesitated.

His throat felt dry, and his voice sounded raspy. He sat up slowly. His eyes finally took in his surroundings. It looked like a typical hospital room, but everything felt different—slow and hazy, as if his brain were soaked in molasses. His thoughts seemed fuzzy. He cleared his throat before trying to speak.

"Hello!" He pushed the call button and waited for a nurse, but no one came. He attempted to yell again, but still no response.

He slid down off the bed, a little wobbly on his feet at first. He slowly walked toward the door, then struggled to pull it open, but the knob wouldn't turn. His hand slipped right through the doorknob, and he backed up in fear.

As he looked at the bed, he turned pale. He saw himself, lying on the hospital bed, eyes closed, with a slight furrow on his brow.

"What the hell!" he screamed and ran back to the door. He tried to open it again, but nothing happened. He was still in the room—both standing there and lying on the bed.

"Fuck, I'm dead." He began pacing back and forth. "I'm dead. Did I actually pass on?" he screamed in frustration, hoping this was just a bad dream. It couldn't be real. He wondered why he couldn't remember anything. He felt lifeless.

He sprinted back toward the door, and this time he opened it and saw a wide tunnel. The ground felt wet and muddy. He didn't have any shoes on and wore a hospital robe. The walls looked blood red.

Darkness descended, and the smell became so horrible, he started choking. With each breath he took, the foul smell went up his nose, to the point that he tasted the pungent odor. When he turned to go back, the door had disappeared.

He continued down the hallway and heard the cries of people being tormented. He felt as if his body were on fire, and the farther he walked, the more agony and pain he felt. He turned to go back, but there was no place to go. Behind him, all was void and emptiness. He paused and tried to regroup.

Yet his thinking remained slow and hazy. He fell on his knees and, in the distance, heard Nina's voice: *"Wake up, Jonathan. Please wake up."*

He felt certain that this could be his final walk to a prepared place in the abyss.

He heard awful screaming voices and felt evil forces moving inside the tunnel. He kept turning around, looking for a way back. He fell to his knees again, lightning flashed, and everything went silent. His body had been reduced to ashes. He opened his eyes and found himself back in the hospital room.

Jonathan looked around the room and saw the police officer who had been ripped apart by his dogs Thunder and Lightning; Sharon's father, James, whom Jonathan had shot three times; 174 people burned alive in a drug house; Linda's father and his friend shot three times each; Frankie J, his father, with a broken neck; and 48 other people, including his half-sisters and stepmother, two detectives, and Tommy and Rico, killed by a bomb Jonathan had set to collapse a house. Also, five boys from Attleboro, Massachusetts, each shot three times. A total of 232 people, dead by his own hands.

Deep in his soul, Jonathan felt that he was wrong for the suffering he had caused. *I'm truly the evilest.*

He heard muffled, unrecognizable sounds, as if something or someone were in the room with him, yet out of reach.

He stood next to his body. He followed the tubes and wires to the machines they were attached to. He listened to their horrible sounds, as they forced him to stay alive. He had no sense of time. He started shaking his body but saw no movement.

Then he felt a warm presence in the room, as the ceiling slowly opened. Four bright lights, black, gray, yellow, and white, in the form of humans surrounded him.

"What do you want?"

There was no answer.

"Where am I?" Jonathan asked.

Still no answer.

He didn't want to react, but he watched the human forms of light moving closer to him. He felt the temperature get hotter. He realized that he might not be dead, and that's when the lights rushed him. They savagely beat on him, and he felt every blow.

Jonathan started fighting back, but they had an advantage, because these lights could punch him and then disappear.

"Stop! Why am I here?"

"You don't know?" It was a voice of a female.

Jonathan looked around the room, and a large figure, much bigger than the others, walked toward him and looked him up and down.

"If I'm not dead, where am I?"

"In your mind."

"What? I don't understand. I want out. What happened to me?" He tried to remember but couldn't force his brain to work.

"You aren't dead, if that's what you're thinking," said a soft woman's voice. That's when all of the people he'd killed disappeared.

"Ahh!" He turned around to the sound of the voice but didn't see anything. "Who . . . who is there?"

"Don't be afraid, Jonathan."

"Who are you?"

"The real question is, who are you?"

"Don't give me that bullshit. Show me who you are, now!"

"I think it's time we see who you really are."

Suddenly, the room turned pitch black. The sounds of the hospital faded away, and only Jonathan's heavy breathing remained.

"What do you want?" he yelled. "I'm not afraid!"

"Aren't you? Black, the color of death."

He felt a sharp sting across his face. He stumbled backward, heart racing and fear rising in his chest. Someone punched him again, in the ribs this time, and he doubled over.

"Focus!" the woman yelled.

After two more hits to his body, Jonathan moved enough to successfully dodge the blow from the invisible opponent. Then the room lightened slightly. He tried to focus. He tried to concentrate. He steadied his breathing because he knew, *Everything starts with how you breathe*. Nina told him that all the time, whether he was having sex, fighting, or running: *Control your breathing and control your thoughts*.

He didn't know how, but he blocked the next attack. With each block and each hit, the room continued to lighten. After he landed a fatal blow to his opponent, the room flooded in gray.

"It seems you want to live. Gray is the color of security. Are you safe, Jonathan? Gray can drain you of energy."

Yet again, the attacker pushed him, as he fell to the floor. The attacker had the form of a gray human.

This time, Jonathan was more prepared. He couldn't die. He fought harder. A light sheen of sweat dripped down his face, his breathing hard but controlled. The gray light lifted, and a harsh yellow light bathed the room.

"You think you have the power to decide who lives and dies? Yellow, the color of cowardice."

"I can play your game, too!" he yelled. "Yellow can also mean optimism, honor, and loyalty. I know some things, too, lady. I'm not a fucking coward! I do what's necessary!"

Again, he fought his yellow opponent, this one considerably stronger than the last. This one took much more energy and strength than the other. Jonathan's heart pounded out of his chest, his breathing labored. And suddenly it was over.

White light flooded the room. He remembered, *The white light came from the ceiling. I became paralyzed as the light pulled my lifeless body to the ceiling when I was ten. After I was raped by Lisa.*

White, the color of purity. The color of rebirth.

"Did you think that we were going to let you get away with your killing and your behavior?"

"Go fuck yourself."

"You don't seem to understand the gravity of the situation."

"I understand very well. They hurt me and I hurt them. I am a killer."

"Excellent! Impressive, you have a good sense of self. I believe you know who you are. But are you sorry?"

"Sorry?"

Jonathan's body stiffened, and he fell to the ground. Slowly, his body rose, higher. The higher he rose, the brighter the light became. He felt a soft pressure on his stomach and an even softer whisper in his ear, the words "I love you."

"You fought well. But I'm afraid you're not ready yet."

His body dropped onto the bed, and his eyes flew open. A flurry of nurses rushed in, as he got a brief glimpse of people around him, before they drugged him again and his eyes closed.

Then it all went dark.

The next time he opened his eyes, everything looked fuzzy. His body felt sore. Nina lay on his stomach, and Thunder was in bed with him.

"Nina."

"Jonathan, you're awake."

Thunder licked his face, "Okay, boy, stop, I'm okay."

Nina said, "I'm going to get the doctor."

Jonathan looked around the room and saw his Uncle Duke and Judy.

"Hey, baby bro. Glad you're back."

He strained to speak. "Judy, you look great."

"Thanks, but don't talk too much."

"How long have I been out?"

"Seven days."

The doctor can into the room. "Welcome back, son. I'll run some tests."

The doctor completed his examination, and the nurse took off his restraints.

"Mr. Russo, you're fine. We'll get you walking and give you something for the pain, and you should be out in few days."

"Now that I know you're conscious, baby brother, I have to get back to New York," Judy said.

She kissed him and left.

Jonathan still felt confused about what had happened.

"Nina, I need a word with my uncle. Please take Thunder home."

"Okay, baby, I love you."

Uncle Duke asked, "Do you remember the boy you beat half to death in high school?"

"Darrell?"

"Well, Darrell is Timothy."

"What! I don't understand."

"His mother moved him here, in fear that he would be killed by Tommy and Rico. You had beaten him so bad that he had plastic surgery."

"But he's white."

"All I can say is, the Alabama sun can change a person."

"Shit!"

"He tried to kill you. So I ask this one time: What do you want me to do?"

Jonathan tried to think. He'd known that Timothy looked familiar.

"Uncle, do nothing. He gets a pass."

"Okay, I'm going back to New Jersey."

"Uncle Duke, thanks for being here."

"No problem, kid."

After two days, Jonathan was up and moving around. While he and Nina sat in the hospital room, the dean of student affairs, Dr. William Sapp, and the football coach arrived.

"Glad to see you on your feet, son," Dr. Sapp said.

"Thank you."

"You played one great game. I hope to see you on the field next year."

"We will see."

"We appreciate you."

"Thank you for stopping by."

"Okay, son," Dr. Sapp said. "Take care of yourself."

The doctors told him that he would have chronic pain in his shoulder and neck, probably for the rest of his life. They gave him a strong pain medication. Jonathan finally left the hospital.

Later, as he and Nina lay in bed, she asked, "What happened in those days you were in the coma?"

"There was a war going on in my mind."

"I know. You were moving, and your body was thrashing around like you were fighting somebody, so they had to tie you down. Who were you fighting?"

"Myself. Nina, I just want to be happy. I want to change. But . . ."

"But what, baby?"

"Nothing."

"Why won't you talk to me? Tell me. I can take it. We've been through so much."

"I know. I'm just glad to be here with you."

"Me, too. The thought of losing you hurts me. But I have to go back to New York for more treatments."

"How are you feeling?"

"Better."

"By the way, did you call my uncle and Judy?"

"Yes, they had to know."

"Why was the dog there?"

"He kept walking around campus, looking for you. He somehow made his way to the VA Medical Center."

"My dogs! I love my dogs!" he said proudly.

Lightning ran into the room, jumped on the bed, and barked uncontrollably.

"Now what?"

Jonathan followed Lightning into the other room, where the dogs stayed. Lightning climbed on top of Thunder and started howling. Jonathan walked over and couldn't feel the dog's pulse. He looked at Nina sadly, and she started to cry.

"What am I going to do? Lightning won't last without him."

Thunder and Lightning's puppies ran out the back door. Jonathan didn't chase them; he just let them go.

He watched Lightning. She licked his face, climbed on top of Thunder, and then died.

Jonathan's two best friends were gone. He buried them in the back yard at 309 Barrow Street two days before Thanksgiving.

It was a long road for Jonathan, but he managed to finish Tuskegee Institute and get a master's degree at New York University by age twenty.

He actually felt happy to leave Alabama. He had some good memories. He put his car and some of his guns in storage, then flew back to New York to start his new life.

He bought a place on Central Park West and established a nonprofit called Creative Resource for Self-Reliance. Its mission was to help children pay for college. He put $50 million of his own money into the nonprofit company and didn't turn any applicants down.

EIGHTEEN

After graduating, Jonathan stayed in touch with his friend Zoe, whom he'd met at the University of Alabama a few years earlier when he tried out for the football team. He visited her about once a month on campus. He enjoyed her company. She was one of those ladies who always had to stay in shape. Yet Jonathan grew concerned because of her excessive drinking and drugging, which were destroying her.

After college, Zoe moved to New York City to work for an investment banking firm on Wall Street. She had an extraordinarily active and creative mind, which made her a great bond trader on the government bond desk. She earned about $250,000 a year, along with a $2 million bonus. After a year of standout performance, she was fired for allegedly stealing $5 million from the bank's customer accounts. Her manager claimed she had found a flaw in the bank's computer system that moved the bank's money into her account. They really didn't know who did it, but because Zoe was the only senior managing trader in the government section, they fired her. The banking officers wanted her in jail, but her father used his influence to keep her from going to prison. The investigators couldn't prove that she did it, but they had to blame someone.

Jonathan planned to meet Zoe for drinks at Rell's Lounge and Grill, on 53rd Street and Park Avenue. As he approached the bar, he looked in the window and saw her doing shots. He walked inside and sat next to her. She didn't look at him.

"May I help you?" the bartender asked.

"Yes, I would like a double Jack on the rocks."

"Nice," Zoe said, as she grabbed Jonathan and kissed him on the lips. She looked into his eyes. "I will always love you."

"Hey, Brown Eyes, what's up with you?"

She smiled. "You're still calling me *Brown Eyes*."

"Always and forever."

"So, what do you think about this situation?"

"It's not good. Did you take the money?"

She gave a helpless shrug. "To be perfectly honest with you, I can't remember."

"Is there a record?"

"Yes. The investigators told me that all transactions were traced back to my computer."

"What did you say?"

"It's an embarrassing situation. I didn't say anything. What could I say?"

She didn't look well. She handed Jonathan a letter from her mother. Jonathan opened and read it.

Dear Zoe, I'm writing this little note to you today because my heart is heavy. I can't talk to you face-to-face because I don't like the paranoia and negative attitude I get from you. I know you're still drinking and doing drugs and acting stupid in the street. I want to ask you why you do the things you do, but I believe you don't know yourself or you lie to me. You don't remember half the things that you do. You need help now, and no amount of talking can convince you until you make up your mind to get help. I'm heartbroken and disappointed because you're an alcoholic and you just keep drinking like an asshole. Sure, life is hard, but it can be beautiful, and you can only see beauty through sober eyes. Everything and everyone turns ugly when you're drunk. You have a beautiful personality, you have a good education, and it seems like you don't even care about any of it. You're probably thinking, "Why is she saying anything to me?

*I'm doing fine. I graduated from a great college and
am doing better than my brother or sister." I'm proud
of you for that. However, your inability to control your
drinking casts a dark shadow over my feelings for you.
Please accept this letter as constructive criticism and get
your act together! Even if you don't accept this letter, I
feel better for writing it.*

Jonathan lowered his eyes and folded up the letter. He felt sad, not
because of her situation, but because he wished he had a mother who
cared, who could see beyond his bullshit. He gave the letter back to her,
and she kept her head down. Tears fell from her eyes, as she ordered
another drink.

"So, what happened?"

"I'd just come off a two-day drinking binge. When I went to work,
the manager of the bank called me into the office. I thought I was being
promoted."

She took another sip of her drink. "Carl, the office manager, asked
me what was going on in my life. He asked about the drinking. He told
me that I needed help. Then the missing money came up."

"Did you deny it?" Jonathan asked.

"Yes. Then he yelled at me and told me that it wasn't about the
money. It was about my life and my self-respect. He told me that I
didn't care about anything or anyone. He said the same bullshit: he
had a business to run and he didn't have time to babysit my ass. I told
him to fuck himself. Then I quit."

"Wow!"

"Anyway, there wasn't much more to say, because at that point,
there were no words, no schemes, and no lies that would win my job
back. In fact, it didn't even hit me that I needed help. Fuck that job,
fuck Carl, and as far as I'm concerned, he can kiss my ass." She tossed
her head, a rebellious look in her eyes. "Anyway," she added playfully,
"I don't need anybody. My daddy has money."

"Why don't you come to a party with me tomorrow?" Jonathan
asked. "It would be good for you. It's a political fundraiser. A lot of

powerful people will be there. They can help you get back on track with your career."

In the two months since Jonathan's nonprofit Creative Resource for Self-Reliance had opened, he had made a lot of important contacts.

"Sounds good to me. I'm back in New Jersey, same address. My parents are out of town. They won't be back for a few weeks."

"See you tomorrow around five. How are you getting home?"

"I'll take a cab."

They kissed, and Jonathan left the bar.

When he arrived at Zoe's house the next day, she invited him in.

"This house is amazing."

"Welcome."

Jonathan noticed that she had been drinking. Her eyes were red, and she slurred her speech.

"What are you doing?" Jonathan shouted. "Why are you drinking? You know how important this night is for you."

"Please knock it off," Zoe said. "I'm okay. I just had a glass of wine. Why the fuck are you yelling at me anyway?"

She started crying. "This is my life, and I can't change. I must get high to stay alive, because if I stop, I believe that I will surely die."

"Bullshit. Keep telling yourself that. I think you need help, and after tonight you should get it. Zoe, I need you with me tonight. This is important to you. Don't fuck this up."

"Please get off my back," Zoe said. "You're just like my father."

"What? What the fuck did you say to me?"

"Why are you so angry?"

"You really need this. Do you get what I'm trying to do for you? I'm angry because you're messing up your life. You're a beautiful lady."

"Yeah, whatever. I promise. I'm going to finish dressing."

"Look! Don't whatever me. Your promises are like the smell of dog shit in the winter. The promises are gone as soon as they are made."

"Fuck you."

"Really, that's how you feel?"

"You know, Jonathan, you're nothing more than a bitch boy."

"You think I'm a fucking coward. Is that what you think?"

As he looked into her brown eyes, he remembered all of the fun they'd had together. He wanted the old Zoe back.

"Yeah! I think you're a fucking pussy."

Jonathan didn't move. He felt paralyzed, a little boy again. All he could do was think of his sisters, led by Judy, physically beating and verbally abusing him.

"You're a grown ass man, and you really need to stop acting like a child. So, let's fuck."

She took off her robe, and Jonathan looked her up and down. He didn't want her anymore. She didn't look well. She'd lost a lot of weight, and she appeared sloppy.

"Listen, I'm only going to say this once."

She interrupted him. "You're just a fucking chicken." She slapped him in the face. He backed away, and she said, "I told you that you're just a bitch boy. You don't have the balls to hit me back."

"Stop!"

"Stop what? Hit me! Go ahead and hit me. Prove to me that you're a man."

She fell on the floor.

"Come on, baby, get up. It's going to be okay."

"Come fuck me first."

Zoe got up, walked to the bar, and finished two shots of gin. She went into the bathroom, and Jonathan followed her.

"I'm your friend, and all I want to do is help you."

"Well, go fix me another drink, bitch boy."

"You know I can't take this shit anymore."

Zoe reached over and slapped his face again. He fell to the floor. She tried to kick him, but she missed. He didn't want to hurt her, so he ran to another room and slammed the door. She kicked the door open and threw a vase at him. It hit him in the head, and he chased her. When he caught up to her, he threw her down and pinned her to the floor. He stared at her for a few seconds. He wanted to kill her. The anger he felt made his blood boil. He thought of all the reasons why he should end her life. He felt pissed that he'd allowed her to make him feel like a child again.

"Get off. Get the fuck off."

Jonathan got up and walked away.

"Come back here, bitch boy, I'm not done yet." She ran after him. When she saw the blood dripping down his head, she stopped.

"Shit, I'm sorry."

She reached out to touch his head, but he moved away. She ran crying into the bathroom.

When Jonathan went to check on her, she had passed out on the bathroom floor. He picked her up and put her into bed, thinking, *I have no idea why she stole the money. Her parents are millionaires seventy-five times over.*

He sat in the chair and watched her sleep.

She woke up around ten in the evening.

"Hey," Zoe said.

"You okay?"

"No, I feel like an idiot."

"As you should," Jonathan said.

"Sorry."

"I thought I was special to you."

"You are."

"You need help."

"Why are you giving me such a hard time? Knock it off!"

"I have a lot on my mind. I don't need us. Like this."

Zoe started to cry and said, "I understand. You're like everyone else, you just want to leave me."

"That's not it."

"Sorry I spoiled your night and sorry for calling you a bitch boy."

"I forgive you. Please get some help."

"I'll try."

"That's all I ask."

Jonathan kissed her and went to the party alone.

NINETEEN

One Thursday morning around 3:30 a.m., Jonathan was driving on the Grand Central Parkway near LaGuardia Airport. The weather was cool, with a light spring breeze. He enjoyed driving around before the traffic picked up. It helped him think. He pulled the car onto Runway Drive near the northeast runway, number forty-four. He had to relieve himself. He saw two men walking toward him.

"Can you help us?"

"What do you want?" Jonathan asked.

"A few dollars."

"I don't have it."

"Come on, man, be a sport."

"Please go away," Jonathan said. "See what you made me do? I pissed on my pants. Asshole!"

They look like Mexicans, he thought and wished his dogs were there.

One of the guys pulled out a knife.

Jonathan just looked at him. "I know you're kidding, right?"

"We just want the money."

Jonathan reached into his pocket and gave them $200 to avoid any conflict.

"I know you got more."

"I gave you money. Walk away."

"No, you might go to the police."

"Go away."

One of the guys said, *"Matar a ese negro."* ("Kill that black.").

"Please, I asked you to walk away."

As they approached, he didn't hesitate. He pulled out his gun and shot the first guy, two in the heart and one in the head. The other guy ran. Jonathan shot him in the leg.

"No, don't kill me, please, sir, have mercy."

"From asshole to sir, I wish I could have mercy." Then he reloaded and fired two in the heart and one in the head. It was the first time he felt remorse.

He got back into his car and started driving on the West Side Highway, heading home to 360 Central Park West. He saw a woman walking on the side of the highway. Jonathan thought it strange to see anyone walking in this area at this time of the morning—or, for that matter, at *any* time of the day.

He slowly pulled the car alongside her. "Hey, lady, do you need help? Do want me to call the police?"

She moved closer to the window and asked, "Can you give me a ride to my apartment?"

She looked wet and dirty, but she wore expensive clothes. He didn't want her to get into the car. He would have preferred to call the police. He took a blanket out of the trunk and wrapped it around her. Her body felt cold to the touch, as he helped her into the passenger seat.

"Where do you want to go?"

"Central Park East." She gave him the address.

"What's up with you?"

She didn't say a word.

Jonathan merged onto the highway. "Are you going to talk to me?"

"I don't know what to say."

"Say anything. Don't be depressed, you're an attractive woman. Just get it off your chest. What's your name?"

"Ashira. Ashira Freeman."

"What a nice name, Ashira."

"Yours?"

"Jonathan. Where do you work?"

"I'm a lawyer."

"Very nice."

"This is a great car. It rides well, and it's roomy and spacious."

"It was a gift."

Jonathan waited for her to say something, but she sat there with her eyes closed and her head down.

"So, do you want to tell me what's up with you?"

She paused for a few minutes and then started crying. Jonathan wasn't sure whether he should take her to the hospital.

"Do you have family here?"

"No. I want to tell you something."

"I'm here for you. Anything. Maybe I can help you. Just tell me."

"You're the nicest man," she said. "Well, I went to the overpass and jumped. I wanted to die and still do.

"I believed that I could fly. The idea was in my mind. However, my body didn't agree. Every now and again, and more and more each minute of the day, the pain of loneliness grows to the point where I just don't ever feel good. Even when the time calls for me to be happy, laugh at a good joke, or meet an old friend, I can't. It's because I have so much to handle, and the only answer, at the time, would be to end my life. So tonight I jumped, and my body hopelessly and helplessly fell into the river, without any effort on my part, other than choosing to put myself in that position. The water was cold."

"Wow!"

"My life is hard, and I felt driven to achieve, and it made me crazy. I did extremely well, as far as money is concerned, but my life is a horror show, with many sequels and prequels. Anyway, I knew it would be over soon, as my body sank. I accepted that I was dying and the pain would be over soon. The pain would finally go away. But I noticed that there were no white lights, no angel of mercy, and no spiritual beings coming to take me away. There was no stairway to heaven or man at the gate, looking up my name in the book. There was no elevator to hell. When I opened my eyes, everything was dark and thick. I couldn't see in front of or behind me. Nonetheless, I could feel the trash that filled the river. I couldn't smell the odors of life but instead tasted the bitter, nasty, murky waters. Talk about gloom and doom. I couldn't hear, but I knew the happy and sad sounds of life. In only a matter of time, I would be dead. I realized that I was truly alone. If I had been on the train on my way to work, at least people would be around me. I was truly alone, and I would die alone. Nobody would know me or who I am. Mostly, nobody would care. When my body surfaced to the top of the river, it would be deteriorated, my face would be faded, and my soul would be morally corrupted.

"Is this my legacy? Newsflash: *Person dies alone.* Do I have to die now? If God led me to this bridge last night and told me to jump, then when did I start listening to God? Although I prayed for a better life, it never happened. It's cold and lonely, really lonely, sitting here, waiting to die. Where are the angels? It's all a lie. Not only am I alone in life, will I be alone in death?"

"This is so sad," Jonathan said.

"Sons of bitches on television, talking about the lights or seeing their bodies lying there, while they float around in space. Fuck an 'out of body' experience. It's a lie. When I saw that there were no lights, no stairway to heaven or highway to hell, I wanted to go back to living and try to make it better. I swam to the top, and when I got there, the sun was shining. I now believe that when God tells his angels to come get me, then and only then will I see the true light."

"That was an amazing event for you!" he said, while thinking, *Lights, how I remember the lights.*

"Jonathan, I just want to be me."

"I'm not sure I understand."

"Never mind. Here's my apartment."

They exchanged numbers.

"I could love you," she said.

"We'll talk later."

Jonathan drove off, muttering, "Fuck me! Every woman in my life is a pain in the ass!"

TWENTY

Jonathan walked into Memorial Sloan-Kettering Cancer Center and headed up to Nina's room. She lay in bed, sleeping. Her hand rested on the morphine drip button—she called it "the red button." She was on ninety milligrams of morphine every two hours.

He'd gotten her the best care money could buy. Her health care bill had topped $150,000. She had a private room. But nothing more could be done.

Ovarian and breast cancer had ravaged her body. She continued to deteriorate at a rapid rate. He sat down in the chair next to her bed.

"Nina, wake up." Jonathan slowly rubbed her hand. "Wake up."

"John John, is that you?" she asked softly.

"Hey, Trixie."

"Hey. Look under my pillow and take my book. It's my address book and pictures. I want you to have it. I don't have much to leave you."

"You're leaving me with some wonderful memories. I want to tell the world how I feel about you, with all the amazing things you did for me. We had great hopes for no more sorrow. I'm so heartbroken that we wouldn't be together. Our dreams would have come true. I love you, Nina, and I hope it stays that way. I'll dream that special dream, so that I will never forget you."

"You sure are a romantic. Do you have any candy? My mouth is so dry."

He gave her some candy. She tapped the bed, indicating that she wanted him to get in with her. She moved over a bit and adjusted her body. He noticed how much weight she had lost.

"Hi."

"Hey." As he looked into Nina's eyes, he saw a shell of a person. He whispered in her ear, "I need you to do me a favor."

"I'm not sure how, but whatever you like."

He moved closer to her ear and murmured, "Tell God I'm sorry from the bottom of my heart, and I'm sorry that I hurt so many people."

"What? What are you saying? You're the nicest man I know."

"I'm evil. I did things."

"No, you're the best, and you need to believe that. Do you want to talk about it?"

"No. I want to spend time with you. It's just us." Jonathan knew he could never reveal his secrets, even to someone on her deathbed.

He snapped out of the "feeling sorry" mode and said, "Please, just tell God I'm sorry."

"Okay. Now pray for me," Nina asked.

"Dear God, I want you to know that I'm so sorry that I hurt so many people. It weighs heavy on my mind from time to time, but I have come to realize that I cannot change the past. Forgive me and Nina. Comfort Nina and take her into your loving arms. Amen."

"Okay," Nina said. "Now do something for me."

"Anything." He reached over and touched her hair, which was slowly falling out. *She is so beautiful. I can't image what my life would have been like if she'd never told those sisters, "Leave him alone, he's too little for you to be beating on him." Nina took a brutal beating from Judy that day, which changed my life.*

"The pain is getting worse," Nina said. "I can feel myself dying inside. I can't eat or sleep. I want this pain to stop, and no amount of medication helps. I wish we could share a meal together. I wish we could share our bodies together. I want to feel again, even if it's only for a moment. I want to know that before I take my last breath, love is still in my heart. I want you to kiss me and hold me, so that I can remember how it feels to be held and loved. I know that I'm going to be all right. I will be in a better place. For the time I have left in the world, every moment in my life is yours. I need you to do this for me, Jonathan. I need it."

"I love you so much," Jonathan said. "Don't leave me, please don't leave me. I want to hold you all day. I don't want you to go. We've been together so very long. You have trusted me with your heart."

Tears flowed down his face, and he kissed and hugged her.

"Mr. Lover Boy." Nina smiled. "Stop crying. Do you want to know something?"

"What?"

"I love you, too."

"I'm really going to miss you."

"I will be with you always, even when you're fucking your nasty girlfriends." They both laughed. "Also, in your heart. When you need me, close your eyes, and I will be there. You're a good man."

"Love you."

"The one thing that I wish would have happened is that we'd had a child together," Nina said. "Now kiss me."

While kissing her, he heard the beats from the electrocardiograph getting slower. He stopped kissing her.

Her eyes closed, and she said, "I love you. I love you."

A few moments later, the beeping stopped. With her eyes still closed, she said, "I love you." Those were her last words.

Jonathan cried out, "I love you!"

Nurses and doctors rushed into the room but couldn't do anything to save her. The doctor called the time of death.

Jonathan went into the hall and fell on his knees.

A social worker and one of the doctors helped him up and took him to the social worker's office. She poured two glasses of scotch. Jonathan couldn't talk just yet. He needed to regain his composure.

"I'm Dr. Deena Berman. I'll try to help you."

Jonathan got himself together. "My emotions are lost. I can't feel anything. Why can't I feel anything?"

"You might not believe this, but you're going to be alright. For now, allow yourself to go through the grieving process. You're in shock. That's why you can't feel."

"I want to die, but I don't want to die. You know what I mean?"

"As you start to adjust to life without Nina, your life will become a little calmer and more organized. Eventually, you'll be able to think about your loss without pain and sadness. You will once again anticipate good times to come, and you will even find joy."

Jonathan listened to every word she said.

"How long have you guys been married?" Dr. Berman asked.

He had trouble speaking. "We were not married."

"Really. How old are you?"

"I'm twenty, and she was twenty-eight."

Jonathan told Dr. Berman that they'd lived in the same household. They talked for hours, about life and where he was going from there.

He opened Nina's book and found pictures of him coming out of the woods with the wolf pack in Montana. He never forgot what he'd learned in the woods. He could see Nina's face when he came out of the woods and how happy she looked to see him. She had also saved pictures of him playing football.

"Did she have family?"

"Her father, Tommy, was killed in a fire."

"That's sad."

"I'll talk to Nina's sister to find out where her father's buried. I would like her to be near her father."

After Jonathan left the hospital, he swallowed a couple of pain pills and bought a bottle of cheap wine. He took a taxi to Central Park and sat on a bench there.

He walked the long way back to his apartment at 360 Central Park West.

He thought, *There were times in my life when I felt alone, but never like this. It hurts. Nothing in the world can prepare you for the death of the love of your life.*

He noticed a couple holding hands as they walked through the city streets in the cool morning air.

When he got home, he looked around, and it felt cold. *There's no feeling in this apartment.* He walked over to the bar, fixed himself a drink, and took some more pain pills. He hoped that he wouldn't sink into a deep depression over Nina's death.

Life was short, and he wanted to focus on the good times. He believed that he would be okay, but he knew that he had to stay focused.

He looked around Nina's room and found more pictures of them together and some papers. In her jewelry box, he saw all of the nice things he'd bought for her. He noticed a birthday card he'd given her nine years ago. He found a letter addressed to him.

> *Dear Jonathan, I truly love you. I can't imagine my life these last few years any other way. All I am is because you took care of me. So, if you are reading this, then cancer took my life. But that's okay. I accepted death a long time ago.*
>
> *You can give my jewelry away, if you like, and anything in my room. Please don't keep it and torture yourself.*
>
> *Do you remember the first day you made love to me? It was a good day. I wished we were together more. Hey, be strong and handle your business. I know you like to help people, but be careful of the people you help. Not everyone has your best interests at heart. I know that you did things in your life. Don't worry about it.*
>
> *Keep moving—keep a clear conscience, in other words—and don't tell anybody shit. You'd end up hurting more people than you counted. The truth hurts, and not many people can handle the truth. Keep it to yourself, and if you feel like telling someone, talk to me or talk to God. I love you with my whole soul.*
>
> *Nina*

Jonathan found Tommy's other daughter listed in Nina's address book and called her.

"Hello, my name is Jonathan Russo."

"Hi. What can I do for you?"

"Well, I called to inform you that Nina, your sister, passed away today." He heard her crying on the other end of the phone.

There was a pause, an awkward silence.

"Are you there?" Jonathan asked.

"Yes. I was wondering why I hadn't heard from her."

"She was very sick and in a lot of pain."

"You know, I think we met a while ago in the park. My father, Tommy, would take us to the park all the time. You were just a baby."

"Can I come over? I need to talk to you."

"Sure. I'm in Brooklyn."

"I'll be there in one hour."

He felt nervous as he rang the doorbell. A lady answered the door, about five-six, nice shape, but he could tell that life hadn't been kind to her. She looked forty but might have been no more than twenty-nine years old.

"Hi, I'm Jonathan."

"I'm Betty. Sit. Do you want a drink? I have wine."

Jonathan looked around and saw photos of himself when he was a little boy and pictures of Nina. Tears came to his eyes—not because of Nina, but because he truly loved and missed Tommy. He got up to examine the pictures.

Betty came back into the living room with the bottle and a corkscrew. He opened the bottle and poured them two glasses of wine.

Betty asked, "How old were you in that picture?"

"Nine."

"You were so small."

"I came by because I wanted to ask you where Tommy was buried."

"Why?"

"I would like to bury Nina next to him. If it's okay with you."

"Sure, I'll get you the information before you leave."

"Did Tommy have any other kids?"

"After Anna, he gave up women."

"So my stepmother's daughter was my girlfriend." They both laughed. "He gave up on women—yeah, right!"

"Don't act like you didn't know he was gay."

"If that made him happy, then there's no problem, I guess."

Betty told him that Tommy and Rico had been high-level police officers and were involved in a robbery with Frankie J. They paid off Frankie J to keep him from telling the story to the newspapers. Then they became Frankie J's bodyguards.

"I loved him," Betty said, "but he was never around for me. When I did see him, he would talk about you, how he wished that he could have helped you. What did he mean?"

"Long, hurtful story. I'd rather not talk about it."

"Okay. After Tommy died, he left me this house, a car, and a few dollars." She put her hand on his arm. "So, you never got married?"

"No. How about you?" Jonathan asked.

"It's just me and this house."

"Okay, I'll pick you up tomorrow. I'd like to get this over with as soon as possible. I'll call you with details."

The next day Jonathan and Betty made the arrangements and that week had Nina buried next to Tommy.

TWENTY-ONE

"Hi, my baby boy," Brenda said.

"What do you want?"

"That's no way to talk to your mother."

"Again, what do you want?" He truly detested her.

"I need money for your sister Lisa."

"I don't have it."

"Look, you're going help your sister, and I don't want to hear any shit from you."

Jonathan paused.

"You hear me, or—"

Jonathan interrupted, "Or what?"

"Or I will take legal action and tie you and your nonprofit ass up in court for the rest of your life."

"Fuck you, bitch!"

"Fuck me? No, fuck you, asshole."

"Brenda, think very carefully about the next words you say."

"You know you have a family you need to take care of, and I will make sure you take care of your fucking obligations. You hear me? I will make your life a living hell!"

"Call you later."

"You fucking better. Call Lisa, too!"

He hung up the phone. Brenda needed more money. She had spent $900,000, mostly on drugs, and some of the money went to friends. Jonathan also kept getting a lot of grief from Lisa. After he gave her his house in Alabama, she kept asking for more money.

He told himself, "These types of people will never be satisfied. They're greedy and materialistic, and, in itself, there's nothing wrong with that, but they don't care about anyone except themselves. I'll have to deal with them soon, or the situation will get totally out of control. I might have to kill them both."

He wanted to talk to someone about Nina and figured that Renee would be the best person. Renee acted like more of a mother to him than Anna or Brenda would ever be.

"Hello."

"Sharon."

"Who's this?"

"Jonathan."

"Hi. How are you?"

"Not good. Nina died."

"Sorry to hear."

"Where is Renee?"

"She's in Atlanta. My grandmother died."

"Sorry for your loss."

"Where are you?"

"I'm at my place in the city. Why?"

"Can you come see me?" she asked.

"It's not a good time for me. Plus, are you sure it's alright with Tyrone?"

"You don't know?"

"Tell me, because I don't know what goes on in your life."

"Don't be like that. He's in jail for life. He will never get out."

"What do you want me to do about it?"

"Some fucking compassion, maybe! You don't know what's going on in my life, so please give me a fucking break."

"Fine. I need Renee's number. I'll be there later."

She paused and then said, "Jonathan, I never stopped loving you. Please come."

"Later."

Jonathan arrived at Sharon's house around three o'clock in the afternoon. When he saw her, they greeted each other with a hug, but there were no more feelings between them.

"You look good."

"Thanks."

"I know I look like shit. But I'm glad you came."

"So, what's so important that you need to see me?" he asked.

Sharon had been on the phone when Jonathan got there. She handed him her telephone.

"Here, it's my mother."

"Hello, Renee."

"Hi. I'm sorry."

"Thanks. I'm going to be in Atlanta tonight. I'll come see you. I need to deal with my sister. Where are you?"

She gave Jonathan the address of a motel.

"See you later," he said.

"Yes, be there around six."

"Okay." He hung up. "So, Sharon, what's so important that you needed to see me?"

"I just need some money to move. And before you tell me no, I know you've got it because of that big nonprofit you own."

"I don't like to be pushed. How much?"

"Four thousand dollars."

"Let me think about it."

"What?"

"I didn't say no, but I don't have that type of money on me."

"Call me later, okay?"

"I'll be out."

Jonathan turned and walked away from her. He knew he would never see Sharon again.

TWENTY-TWO

After landing at Atlanta International Airport, Jonathan approached a car service driver holding a sign with "Russo" in large block letters. He thanked the man for stopping at the florist's on the way. He slid into the back seat of the full-length white limousine and pushed aside three bouquets of roses: two dozen red and one dozen white, with a pink rose in the middle.

They drove off to Motel 6. Jonathan called Renee to see if she was okay, and she told him she hadn't checked out yet because she didn't have enough money.

When he saw her, he was surprised that she looked so good, standing there waiting for him in a red T-shirt and jeans. She wore her hair in a ponytail. He didn't say a word as they tightly hugged, in a body-crushing embrace.

"Don't let me go," she whispered. "Squeeze every last drop of air out of me."

He held her so tight, the vibration from his arms made her shake.

After a few minutes, she stepped back and looked him up and down.

"You're one fine man. Wow! You look nice. I remember when you were only twelve years old. Look at what the years have done!"

"Thank you. You're sexier than ever."

"That's so sweet. I'm glad you made it. Sorry about Nina, she was such a good friend to me. I know you loved her."

"Yes, very much. I really do miss her so much. I hope she's in God's loving hands and she's resting in peace."

"I know she was very special to you."

Renee said that her friend was wiring her some money through Western Union, because she had run out of money to pay for the motel. She hadn't realized she would be there so long.

"I'll take care of it." Jonathan boldly walked up to the front desk.

He pulled out his wallet and withdrew a black Visa Diamond credit card from Eurasian Bank in Kazakhstan.

The clerk took care of the bill and wished Jonathan and Renee well. They walked over to the limousine, and the driver held the door open. As they made themselves comfortable, he closed the door, got into the front seat, and drove toward downtown Atlanta.

"What kind of credit card is that?"

"A black Visa from a bank in Central Asia."

"Really! So you're going to disappoint me by telling me that you're selling drugs and that's why you have a black Visa?"

"No. I don't deal drugs, I just take them."

"Funny."

"My grandmother left me some land in Montana, and it paid off very well."

"You promise, no drugs. Right?"

Her voice sounded like a little girl's, waiting to be disappointed.

"No, I promise."

"I'm going to trust you on this one."

On the way to the hotel, Renee moved closer to Jonathan and put her head on his chest.

"So, are these flowers for me?"

"No, they're for my girlfriend."

"You're funny. So what do I have to do to get flowers like this?"

"I'm sure we can think of something."

Renee thanked him for the flowers, and then he gave her the watch and a gold rope chain. She slid her arms around his waist and started to cry. He put his arm on her shoulder and held her until she finished. Then he poured each of them a glass of wine.

"Thank you." She took a sip. "This is nice, very sweet."

Jonathan wiped her tears, leaned over, and kissed her.

"Are you trying to make a move on a helpless lady?"

"Yes. Yes, I am."

They both laughed.

Renee held up the gold chain. "Thank you so much."

"I'm glad you like it."

"Wow! I just can't believe how good you look."

"I'm sorry about your mother," Jonathan said.

"Thank you. I know you miss Nina."

"It's hard some days, especially at night. I miss her so much, I just can't imagine how my life will be without her. She's been a constant in my life, and I truly wish she was here today."

"Do you miss your family?"

"No, not really. They're just a bad dream. They paid a price for what they did to me."

"I know, baby. Nina told me."

"I don't really want to talk about it. They hurt me. They're gone, yet I still stand."

"It's going to be all right. You'll see. Give it time. By the way, where are we going?"

"To the Ritz-Carlton. In downtown Atlanta."

She moved away from him. "Stop it. No drugs."

Jonathan said, "Or I can put you on a plane and send you home."

"Okay. Okay, I'll be a good girl."

"Let's have fun and just relax."

"I'm sure you heard what happened?"

"Yeah. Not good. I saw Sharon. She said Tyrone is in prison for life."

After a few glasses of wine, Renee finally relaxed. She told Jonathan that Tyrone had shot two undercover federal agents who had infiltrated his gang. He'd found out that one of his captains, an undercover federal agent, had sex with Sharon and they had a baby boy. When Tyrone confronted him with threats of death, he confessed that there was another undercover agent and could tell Tyrone the name, if Tyrone would let him go. He also confessed that the baby boy was his. Tyrone killed both agents.

After that, the whole power of the federal government came down on him and destroyed his gangs, from Boston to Queens. They arrested everyone. Most of the gang members ended up taking deals, but Tyrone wanted to take everyone to court.

Renee explained that Tyrone made her take out a second mortgage on the house, he destroyed her credit, and she lost her job when they found out that her sister had given him information from law enforcement. Judy was arrested and sent to prison in New York.

"That's some shit. I'm sorry it happened to you and Sharon. Why did your sister get involved with him?"

"Why do you think?"

"Hey, don't get mad at me," Jonathan said. "It's not my fault. She should have known better."

"Sorry, I'm just so fucking pissed off when I think about all the lives that were fucked up. But she did it for the money. He paid her very well. I didn't know that my sister was involved. She told Tyrone about all of law enforcement's moves."

"Have you seen him?"

"Fuck him, I hope he dies in jail and never sees the light of day."

Renee said that Tyrone was in a United States penitentiary in Colorado—a maximum-security facility called the "supermax." He was on lock-down twenty-three hours a day and had one hour of exercise. He had no human contact with anyone, everything was automated, and he could receive only one telephone call a month.

Say what you want about the government, Jonathan thought, *but they protect their own.*

After they arrived at the hotel, Jonathan showed his Visa card, and the entire staff in the lobby rushed over. He rented an executive suite with all of the amenities.

Renee whispered in his ear, "So with this magic card, everyone gives you pretty much anything you want?"

He laughed. "Pretty much."

In their suite, Renee flung herself onto one of the beds, and Jonathan ordered two rib-eye steaks and two salads. They devoured their dinner with minimal conversation, and Jonathan jumped into the shower.

When he emerged dripping wet, Renee was standing there nude, which scared him a little. He checked out her body, as she did his. She brushed past him and got into the shower.

He turned on some soft music and poured two glasses of wine. He sat on the sofa facing the window, which overlooked downtown Atlanta. Renee came out of the bathroom wearing the hotel's terrycloth robe. He handed her a glass.

She took a sip. "This is really good. What is it?"

"Red wine."

"Always joking. No, really."

"Colgin Napa Valley red wine. It's about four hundred dollars a bottle."

"It tastes different."

"That's because you're used to cheap mad dog wine."

"I like it."

After several glasses of wine, Jonathan moved closer to her, leaned over, and called her name. When she turned her head, he kissed her on the lips.

"So, you came all this way to get some pussy?"

"Si."

She put her glass down, looked at him, and moved away. She gazed into his eyes. He closed his eyes, moved in, and kissed her again, and this time, it was a seal—a seal of their relationship, of what was to come. He kissed her as if they wouldn't see each other again. He pushed her away ever so gently and pulled her back. He kissed her again, and this time he went to the bottomless pit of his soul, to come back with how he wanted her to feel about him.

Only her needs and her wants mattered. He concentrated on the way she responded, focusing on how she tasted and her body movements. He thought how good it would be to have sex with her.

"I haven't had sex in over six years. I don't know how it's going to feel. Please don't hurt me."

"Who said we're going to have sex?" he asked jokingly.

She playfully punched him in the chest, "Fuck you! I know you want me!"

"Yes, I do. I really do."

"So, what's the problem?"

"Nothing."

"Just don't hurt me. Okay?"

"We'll go slowly, and when you say stop, I'll stop."

She nodded and then took off her robe. She only had panties on. He slipped out of his robe. He was nude. She climbed on top of him. He loved the way she felt in his arms. She closed her eyes and he kissed her. She didn't utter the sounds he had become so accustomed to hearing. Normally, if he were with a young lady, she would have been crying out his name by now.

He kissed her on the neck, and she kissed his neck and said, "You're so sexy. This feels so fucking good."

Her lips opened wider and her warm breath titillated him. His heart raced. He controlled his breathing. He reached down, ripped off her panties, and put his finger inside her. She bit down into his neck. He continued slowly going in and out of her. He felt her breathing pick up speed. She moved his hand, and Renee sat on him, facing him. She lowered herself onto him and wrapped her legs around him.

He kissed her breasts, and she guided him inside her and moaned softly.

"Don't move, let me do the work."

He nodded. As she started to go faster and Jonathan's body tightened up, he put his head back and let her go to work. He tried to fight the urgent feeling, surprised he was able to continue. He disregarded everything and kept his mind centered on Renee. She was moving too fast.

"Slow down, we have all night."

"I'll try," Renee said.

Jonathan thought, *We're not coordinated. We're acting like two virgins.* So he took control. He concentrated on how she tasted. Her lips soft and tender, her skin soft and warm, her breath with a hint of wine.

"Slow down," he said. "I want you to experience having sex with me. I don't just want to fuck you, I want to love you."

"Okay."

She closed her eyes and screamed out a little, but she was a quiet lover. Jonathan gently bit down on her neck and sucked, and she moaned again. He could feel her heart beating faster. He gave her a long kiss. He could feel her shaking, and she moaned again. Her arms' tight grip around his body loosened, and her body went limp. He began kissing her again, keeping her desire to only what she wanted. He didn't know much about older women, so he just kissed and nibbled all over her body, kissing her neck, earlobes, shoulders, and upper chest.

She got off him, and Jonathan stood, picked her up, and carried her to the bedroom. While walking to the bed, he kissed her again. He put her on the bed and he went down on her. She was so wet and was moving so much that he couldn't keep his lips on her. He grabbed the backs of her thighs and went to work again. He thought, *That should keep her still.*

She grabbed his hair and pulled him in closer and she came. He got up, turned her on her stomach, and entered her. She held onto the headboard, as he moved slow and then fast. He took her to the edge of ecstasy and then stopped. He started again, until he had total control of her. He had never really made love to a woman until this moment. After he felt she was ready, he took her there. He could feel her start to have muscle spasms. She yelled out and pushed him off her. She lay there and then rolled over.

"Wow!"

He reached out to touch her.

"Give me a few minutes."

She kept lying there and didn't move. Then she rolled over, facing him.

"I've never in my life felt this way," Renee said.

They cuddled in silence for a while.

She kissed him. "So, that's what pussy tastes like."

The both laughed.

"Really! Like you never put your fingers down there and got a taste."

She laughed. "You're a nasty boy."

"Sure, I am. Are you okay?"

"Better than okay. Baby, I'm in a state of utter confusion. You've got my mind scrambled."

He winked at her, and she yawned. "I'm going to sleep."

She climbed on top of Jonathan, and he went back inside of her.

"I'll leave you with my favorite signature sexual move of all time, one that will have your head spinning for five days and is world renowned."

"You so fucking crazy. What is it?"

"You ready?"

"Go for it, big boy."

"I'm going to sleep."

"Such an ass."

They both laughed.

"I just want to lie here and not move," Renee said. "Okay?"

"Totally," he said in a relieved voice.

She gave him a long, deep kiss.

"Good night."

"Good night." Within minutes, Renee fell asleep. Jonathan thought about how good it felt to be with her. Then he drifted off to sleep, too.

When he opened his eyes, he saw Renee staring out the window at downtown Atlanta. She sat in a chair with a glass of red wine, her robe hanging off her shoulder.

"Hey."

"Hi."

"Something wrong?"

"No," Renee said.

"What are you doing?"

"Thinking about how all of my adult life I wanted a day like today. A day when I have good male company, good sex, good food, and good conversation, but I never dreamed that it would be with my daughter's old boyfriend. I told you I haven't had sex with anyone in six years. I didn't even think that it still worked."

"So, are you feeling a way about me?"

"No. No. It's that life can be so funny. A few years ago, I put you in the bathtub, and you couldn't have been more than forty pounds. Now look at you, over six feet tall, and what? Two hundred pounds? You're a fine man. Shit! Fucking me like, I don't know. This is the best sex I've ever had, it was more like . . . you knew my body, and you loved my body. You got me." She smiled.

"Well, thank you." Jonathan rolled out of the bed and put a robe on. He poured himself a drink, sat on the floor between her legs, and leaned his head into her lap. She put her leg on his shoulder.

"This is it. This is where I wanted to be all my life. I've never felt this way. It's how you treat and talk to me. Like I'm the only person in the world."

"Do you feel guilty?"

"Fuck no! I would like to believe that after all I've been through over the years, I needed this. I have been alone for so long. First, it was James, who raped me at fourteen and then he raped Sharon."

"Do you ever wonder what happened to him?"

"I know he's dead, because if he wasn't, he would have come back."

"That's the truth."

"Look, I know that nobody in the world can take the place of Nina, but please don't stay alone. There are still a lot of good ladies out there. Or?"

"Or what?"

"Come by and hit me off every now and again."

They both laughed.

In the morning, Jonathan ordered breakfast, and he and Renee took a shower. They had a quickie in the shower and then ate.

She called Sharon to say that she would be home later that day.

When she hung up, Jonathan asked, "Is everything okay at home?"

"Sure."

"Listen, where do you do your banking?"

"Why?"

"I've decided to pay your mortgage and give you money to pay all of your bills until you get a nursing job."

"I don't know what to say. You're sure you are not a—"

He interrupted her. "Be good and don't say it. I told you I made a lot of money from the land deal. I'm set up for life, and I'm going to give you some money."

"Chase."

"I bank there, too."

"Okay."

They got dressed and took the private elevator to the lobby. Jonathan asked his personal hotel concierge to get him a car. The driver took them to downtown Atlanta.

At the bank, Jonathan requested a private banker, and a customer assistance employee, Randy, asked for some identification.

He hit some keys on a computer and did a double take at the screen. "Right away, Mr. Russo."

Jonathan paid Renee's mortgage and credit card bills.

"You changed my life. Thank you."

"Anytime."

At the airport, he said, "Here are my address and keys. I'll be there in two days. I need to take care of some things in Alabama. I hope you're there when I get back to New York."

"I don't know what to say."

He kissed her. She flew to New York, and Jonathan headed off to Alabama.

TWENTY-THREE

Gazing out the window of a private jet, Jonathan reflected on his time with Renee. Although he still mourned Nina, Renee was a great distraction. He thought about life with her, maybe marriage, maybe a baby, and then laughed to himself.

He was flying to Tuskegee to see if he could get Lisa to leave him alone. Or else, he knew he would have to kill her.

His mother, Brenda, had read about his nonprofit organization receiving $10 million from various foundations. In her twisted mind, the money belonged to the family.

After spending his college days at 309 Barrow Street with Nina and burying his dogs Thunder and Lightning there, Jonathan had signed over the property to his sister Lisa.

When he arrived at Bolton Field Airport in Tuskegee, he took a taxi to a storage unit. There, he kept the car Tommy and Rico had bought for him as a graduation gift.

He put on a bulletproof vest and loaded his guns, ready for war. He drove around campus just to reminisce a little and then went down Montgomery Road to Barrow Street.

He parked across the street from the house and saw a little girl sitting on the steps. He looked around and didn't see anybody else.

He grabbed his backpack full of money. Whatever amount he gave Lisa, she could share with Brenda.

The child looked at Jonathan with her big black eyes and then hung her head again. She appeared dirty.

"What's wrong, little girl?"

"Nothing."

"Why are you sitting outside by yourself?"

"I don't know."

"Where is your mommy?"

"She's in the bed."

"Is she sleeping?"

"I don't know."

Jonathan started to lose patience. "Tell me what's wrong."

"My mommy won't wake up."

"Say that again."

"My mommy won't wake up."

"I'm your uncle, Jonathan. I want you to stay here while I check it out, okay?"

"Okay."

"Don't move."

"Okay."

"What's your name?"

"Nikki."

Jonathan mumbled to himself, "Figures Lisa would give her daughter a stripper name."

He cautiously entered the house. It smelled of stale alcohol and smoke. Empty bottles of cheap beer and liquor littered the dining room where he'd once had dinner with Nina. Trash lay all over the place. He checked the first bedroom—a child's room. It smelled of urine.

He pulled out his gun and took the safety off. He checked the second bedroom, and there she was: Lisa. She wasn't moving. Clothing and trash lay scattered around. He moved slowly and walked over to her. He checked her pulse and her breathing. She was dead. He pulled the blanket back to see her body, and her arms were covered with injection marks. He replaced the blanket over her, and relief flooded him.

The message light flashed on the telephone. He walked over and hit play. The caller had phoned last night.

"Hey, Lisa, this is Kara, where the fuck are you? Mommy died. She had a heart attack. Please call me. I've been trying to call you."

That was Lisa's sister Kara. There were several more messages like that. Jonathan let out a deep breath, first feeling disappointment and then happiness. He felt a joy that he'd never experienced before.

He searched the room. There was really nothing in it but old papers and old cheap jewelry. He found Nikki's birth certificate. The birth name on the certificate was Nicole Marie Antoinette Russo. He also found her social security card and packed some clothes for her.

Jonathan went to see his dogs' graves and then walked to the front of the house.

"Nikki, you're going to come live with me, okay?"

"What about my mommy?"

"Mommy's very sick, so I want you to come with me, okay?"

"No! I want my mommy."

"Are you hungry?"

"Yes."

"If you come with me, I'll get you some food."

Jonathan put out his hand, wanting Nikki to take it. He fell on his knees, dropped the backpack, and opened his arms. "Come to me, Nikki."

He closed his eyes and thought about how many times he had been given a second chance and his life had been spared. He thought that if he pulled the trigger and this little girl died, there would be no turning back. There would be no remission of sin.

"I can take you to a better place. A place where you can go to school. A place where you will have a family and there will be other children, but you have to come to me."

Jonathan opened his eyes, and she ran into his arms. He cried, as he squeezed her tight and told her, "It's going to be all right."

He put Nikki in the car and gave her some water. He fastened her seatbelt, and they slowly drove away. He stopped off at the Chicken Coop and bought her a container of chicken nuggets.

He drove north and hours later pulled into Joker Joe's in South Carolina off Interstate 95. While parking the car, he heard a dog barking.

It sounded like Thunder and Lightning. He grabbed the keys,

and they walked over to the café. Inside, he saw Bill. A few years ago, Jonathan had given a puppy to him.

"Big Bill," Jonathan said.

"Hey, my man."

"Nice to see you again. How are things?"

"All is good. I can't complain. Hey, I wanna show you something."

Jonathan took Nikki's hand, and they walked outside. Big Bill went to his truck and pulled out a puppy.

"This is for you."

"Thank you, I really appreciate it."

They headed back to the café and ordered burgers and fries. After eating, they piled into the car again and merged onto the interstate, going north to New York.

Nikki and the puppy played in the backseat until they both fell asleep.

Jonathan arrived in New York City exhausted, with Nikki and the puppy still conked out. He parked the car and carried both of them up to his apartment.

He opened the door and saw Renee lying on the couch. "Hey, I'm glad you're here."

"Who is this?"

"Lisa's daughter. I'll tell you everything later."

Renee helped put the girl to bed.

"Do you want something to eat?"

"You look tired," he said.

"I took some of your sleeping pills."

"Go get some rest."

"I missed you."

"Missed you, too."

"I'm so glad you're here, Renee."

"Me, too."

Jonathan hugged and kissed her and pulled the covers over her and Nikki. He put the puppy on some folded towels.

"Your sister called. She told me to let you know that your mother died. Sorry."

"Thanks."

"You want to talk about it?"

"We could do it later. Go to sleep. I love you, Renee."

"I love you, too, Jonathan."

EPILOGUE

I felt exhausted after that long drive from Alabama to New York. It took me about eighteen hours. I was extremely happy that my dogs Thunder and Lightning had left me a puppy. She will be a testament to their legacy. Thunder, Lightning, and I had a rough start, but in the end, they were my friends, and I'll miss those dogs. I truly love them. I named the puppy Seven.

It's been three weeks since Nina died. When I lost her, I felt as if my heart had been ripped from my chest. Nina was the love of my life. I have a special place in my heart for her. She taught me so much about life. I enjoyed being with her. We helped and protected each other.

About four-thirty in the morning that Saturday, I checked my messages and listened to my sister go on about how our mother had died. I just didn't care at that point.

Now I'm standing in front of my apartment window, overlooking Central Park West. I'm fortunate to have such a magnificent apartment. There aren't many apartments with a great view left in New York City. I have a lot of money. I made the deal of a lifetime, and it made me a rich man. After my grandmother left me that land in Montana, it set me up. I'm now worth approximately seven hundred million dollars. The funds are in various banks around the world. I graduated from Tuskegee University with a Bachelor of Science in Accounting and got a Master in Public Administration and International Development from New York University, all completed within an unprecedented three years. I accomplished more in my twenty-one years than some people do in a lifetime.

Yet at twenty-one, I feel as if I've lived for forty years.

It's five thirty in the morning, and I don't feel good. My emotions are running out of control. I feel alone and scared. It seems like someone is chasing me, but when I turn around, there's nobody there. My mind races all the time, and lately, even though I haven't really slept well most of my life, I've had trouble resting and slowing down my mind. I'm concerned about my well-being. I am in desperate need of some rest. I feel as if I should turn myself in to the police for all of the things I've done and for the people I've hurt. But I'm not sure if that's a good idea because they might not believe my story or they might put me in a mental institution. Anyway, nobody can prove I did anything illegal. Maybe I should blow my brains out, but I'm scared that the gun might not fire or might misfire and paralyze me, so I'm not even sure if that's a good idea.

Although I enjoy most of my life, my past is filled with so much pain. I feel lost and some remorse for the suffering and anguish I caused. I can't break the chains that hold me back from being a better person, because the abuse at the hands of my sisters and my father is very real in my mind.

I fell into my violent lifestyle after being brutally raped at age ten by an older girl, I later found out she was my sister.

Subconsciously, I guess the anger and frustration surfaced because my family tried to break me down and make me conform to their way of life. I had to protect myself.

I realize I can no longer continue this way of life. I need to come up with a way to deal with my problems. I'm trying to tackle one thing at a time, but I still know of only one way to deal with a lowlife person—someone I consider morally unacceptable, who tries to hurt me. Yet truth be told, who made me the judge of who should live or die? Who charged me with the task of destroying families? In the past, I made the decision that somebody had to die, so I pulled the trigger. Who were the targets? The lowlife individuals who exploited others for their own selfish purposes and who hurt the people I loved or cared for or who hurt me. They had to be dealt with, in a manner that I saw fit.

Now it's around six in the morning, and I'm watching the sunburst through puffy clouds. I'm on my second cup of coffee, half-and-half, light with one sugar. I can feel the sun's warmth all over my body as if it's a blanket covering and protecting me. At that moment, looking at the sun, I think about my time in Montana doing the vision quest and the process of restoring my spirit. That quest, being in the woods, living with nature gave me back the very innocence that was stolen from me. Now that I think about nature and the healing of my body and soul, I'm at peace with what happened in my past and what will or will not be.

I now realize that everything has been lifted off my chest. I'm starting to feel much better. Part of me feels empty on the inside because of the things I've done, but I am truly thankful to be alive.

I am starting to get sleepy. I see my dog looking at me, and I pat her lightly on the head and smile. I look at Renee and Nikki sleeping peacefully, maybe for the first time in years.

If I had a chance to do it over again, would I? I've thought about it and said, "I believe that each day has been given to me by the grace of God, and I would not be foolish enough to trade it for another yesterday!"

Out of the smoldering pit of fear come the fresh cooling waters of courage that give me the strength to stand. Yet I still stand. Regardless of the obstacles of this world, I still stand.

The End

Printed in the United States
By Bookmasters